# Can't Stop

**Lauren Biel**

Library of Congress Cataloging-in-Publication Data

Can't Stop/Lauren Biel 1st ed.

Cover Design: Pretty in Ink

Editing: Sugar Free Editing

Interior Design: Sugar Free Editing

For more information on this book and the author, visit: www.LaurenBiel.com

**Please visit LaurenBiel.com for a full list of content warnings.**

*This book is dedicated to the people who see the beauty in what remains*

# Chapter One

### Rayna

Life on the run hasn't been easy, but at least Dalton is good company. It's not as if I was ever used to some sort of normalcy, anyway. Things have been anything but normal since he blew into my world. It's kind of fabulous.

Almost as fabulous as the taxidermy-rat thong I hold against my pants.

"You can't be serious," Dalton whispers. He runs his hand through his dark hair and glares at the bikini bottoms. "They make those to look at, not wear. It's a gag gift."

I peer past him, at the man working the cash register. "Is there a top as well?"

The man grabs a plastic bottle and spits dark liquid into it before raising a gnarled finger toward some shelves in the shadowy back half of the shop. "I think she put some out last week. Ain't been selling too good, so she ain't been making as many."

"Gee, I wonder why," Dalton mutters, and I smack his arm before I head toward the dark recesses.

As I thumb past a raccoon-skin bikini, I find the top that matches the bottoms in my other hand. The stiff skins are barely big enough to cover my nipples, but that's okay. The more Dalton can see, the better. With a grin, I tuck the prizes under my arm and head for the register.

"Eighty-five for the set," the man says, and Dalton begrudgingly pulls his wallet from his back pocket.

It's probably not wise to spend this much money on something so silly, but one day we will put down roots, and when that day comes, I want to have a nice little taxidermy collection started. I'll feather my nest with all the dead things. Van Gogh will still take the top spot, of course, but he needs friends, and this little rat getup is perfect.

Dalton is kind enough to stop at these little hole-in-the-wall shops we pass on our journey south. We have no exact destination in mind. We're just traveling along until something feels right.

Halloween is right around the corner, so that gives me something to look forward to. Dalton thinks we should take the year off, that we shouldn't go on a spree this year. I beg to differ. It's the one time of year when we allow ourselves to indulge in the darkest hobby. We already confine our deeds to a single day per year, and I'm not giving that up.

"He's right, you know," the grizzled man says as he dangles a black plastic bag toward Dalton. "You really shouldn't wear this shit. My wife don't exactly make them with skin-safe ingredients, and I doubt you want to go pressing tanning solution against your nether regions."

Considering the Frankenpeen incident, some aged tanning solution is the least of my concerns. Besides, it's not as if I'll wear it long before Dalton rips it off and ravages me.

I pluck the bag from his hands and thank the man for his advice—which I won't be following—as we leave the shop. My stomach grumbles loud enough for Dalton to hear when we step into the waning fall sunshine. He peers down the strip of stores situated along the edge of a dilapidated parking lot.

"Do you want to try the Chinese place or the Mexican place?"

The Chinese place doesn't even have pictures of the food on the wall, so I opt for Mexican.

Authentic Mexican smells and sounds and sights tease my senses as we step into the building at the end of the strip. A stunning dark-haired hostess leads us to a dimly lit booth in the back of the restaurant. Seconds later, we have drinks and a bottomless basket of chips and salsa.

"Pick something cheap," Dalton whispers as we peruse the menu.

I sigh and pull Van Gogh from my bag. I place him beside the napkin holder with a pat of his head. He's looking a little worse for wear these days, but life isn't easy for this antique squirrel taxidermy. He isn't meant to travel the world.

"We really need to look into setting up somewhere," I say. "We could save the traveling for once a year, when we . . . you know."

Dalton closes his menu and nods. "I know what you mean, bones. I want that too." He reaches across the table and grips my hands. "We just haven't found the right place yet. When we do, we'll know."

He's right. We don't exactly slot nicely into any of the places we've been through so far. We snag odd jobs in the urban and rural communities we pass through along the way, and none has felt like home.

A server comes to take our order. Dalton gets two soft tacos, and I do the same. The chimichangas are calling my name, but I want to have enough money left over to stay some place nice tonight. Preferably somewhere with at least one star.

As we wait for our food, I glance around at the decor, which is mostly placed to set the mood. Papel picado douses the ceiling in color. A large mural depicting a mariachi band performing in a bustling city center dominates the rear wall. But something out of place catches my eye—a large, furry figure in a dark corner. A single dim spotlight illuminates its terrifying and very impossible form.

I snag the arm of a passing busboy and point to the strange taxidermy piece. "Excuse me, what the fuck is that?"

The young man doesn't need to turn his head to know what I'm referring to. "My great grandmother had it commissioned. It's a chupacabra—a legend. She swore that's what it looked like, though, and when she picked it up, she paid extra because the taxidermist did such a good job."

"Can I take a closer look?"

"Rayna," Dalton says.

"What? I won't try to buy it, don't worry." I scoot out of the booth before he can argue further.

The busboy follows me to the strange creature. It looks like a hairless black fox with massive spines protruding from its shoulders and along its back. Sharp, glistening teeth shine from inside its snarling mouth, and its glassy eyes hold so much life despite being both dead and fictional. The craftsmanship is incredible.

The busboy smiles and tucks the empty bus tub under his arm. "You wouldn't be able to buy it. Not for all the money in the world. The man who crafted it lives in some strange town in Florida, and my great grandmother refuses to return there. She called it *ciudad de los muertos*—the city of the dead."

Hmm . . . sounds like my kind of city.

"Why'd she call it that?" I ask.

He shrugs and situates the large gray bus tub on his hip. "Probably because the entire town was obsessed with preserving dead things. Everywhere you looked, something had been frozen in its death state." He shivers and shakes his head. "No, it's no place for people like us."

With that, he walks away, and I return to the table. The food has been brought out, and Dalton has scarfed half of his beans already. I take a seat and shovel a few forkfuls into my mouth to quiet my stomach before pulling out my phone.

"What're you up to, bones?"

Ignoring him, I continue with my detective work and soon discover the name of the city of the dead. As a smirk slides across my face, I turn the phone toward him.

"How do you feel about Florida?"

# Chapter Two

### Dalton

My relationship with Rayna could be likened to a hostage situation. She's unhinged, volatile, and a little mean at times. A rational man would have run for the hills long ago, but she's tethered me to her and refuses to release me. I do her bidding—much to my displeasure at times—because of my undying love for her. I'm a man obsessed.

That's why I'm currently picking my way through the southern section of Virginia as I chart a course toward Oak Hollow in Florida.

I glance over at Rayna. She looks out the window as she fingers the tattered ear on that godforsaken squirrel. He's her comfort object, her most beloved possession. I reach over and slide my hand into hers. Because she's mine.

A figure stands on the side of the road ahead. The man holds a cardboard sign and sticks his thumb toward our car as we approach. Rayna sits a little straighter in her seat when she spots him.

"Couldn't we—"

"No, bones. You know we can't."

She sits back with a little grumble. "Why not? We're currently on the move. By the time they find his body, we'll be in Florida."

The man slides by, and I don't even slow the car.

"Fuck, I'm so bored." Rayna kicks the dash and folds her arms over her chest. "This life was supposed to be exciting. I can't chase a high *only* once a year. It's not enough."

Keeping the kills to one night a year has proven more difficult than we first anticipated. For both of us. She needs the excitement, the adrenaline rush. I need the release. The control.

I spot our exit ahead, so I merge onto the offramp. "What about the activities list? Maybe we could try some of those things. Besides, it's almost Halloween."

We came up with a list of thrilling activities to try throughout our travels. Things that are slightly dangerous or run the risk of getting us caught, but also things that don't have the sort of jail sentence that murder brings.

"Let's fuck on the railroad tracks."

"What?" I nearly merge into a semi as I pull into traffic. "You can't be serious. That wasn't even on the list."

"I'm definitely serious, and I just thought of it. We can make a game out of it. No moving from the tracks until we come."

"Both of us?"

"Yes, both of us. You didn't think I'd let you have all the fun, did you?" She punches something into her phone, and seconds later, she's directing me down side streets.

"So, what . . . we can't kill other people, so we're just going to kill ourselves?"

She grins and tells me to take the next left.

Like her puppet, I oblige. I take the turn, and railroad tracks appear further down a stretch of asphalt that looks like it hasn't seen a pothole repair since its inception. Trees crowd the tracks on both sides, but the lack of growth around the metal ties suggests that trains pass through here regularly. I pull the car to a stop, tucking it off the street and in some brush.

"We can finally play with this!" she says as she pulls something from her bag.

I was wondering when Raul would make an appearance. She stole him from an oddities expo we passed through in Atlanta. It's a possum head attached to a butt plug, and I think it's supposed to be decorative only. That won't stop Rayna from cramming it into her ass and forcing me to look at Raul's glassy death glare while I pound her pussy.

"Must we?" I ask as I unfasten my seatbelt.

"We must."

She climbs out of the car with Raul in hand, and I follow her because I can't help myself. No matter what weird shit she wants to get into, my obsession with her forces me to be her unwilling accomplice. Well, maybe not so much un*willing* as unenthused. I'm always willing to fuck her senseless, even when her strange accessories are involved.

And they usually are.

I follow her down the tracks to where there's a slight bend. I already know where this is going. We won't be able to see the train coming from a distance in either direction, but we'll damn sure hear it and feel the rumble in the tracks.

"Wait!" Rayna holds up a finger and rushes back to the car. When she joins me again, she holds Raul in one hand and Van Gogh in the other.

I open my mouth to ask why, but then I remember who I'm about to fuck on these train tracks. She sets her janky squirrel on one of the rails so he can watch, I guess. Who fucking cares at this point? My brain has officially become commandeered by the prospect of being inside her.

Within seconds, she's on me. A soft moan leaves her lips as her mouth melds with mine. I glance down the tracks as she fingers the hem of my shirt and tries to lift it over my head.

I pull away from the kiss. "Maybe we should leave our clothes on. If we need to get away quickly, it's probably best if we're mostly dressed."

She grumbles and gives up, going for my mouth again.

I can't tear my gaze away from the way the tracks disappear in the distance, though. It doesn't even look like a train could come from such a small place, but it's all an optical illusion. A train will definitely come from that direction. Or head in that direction. Either way, we're directly in its path.

Oh, fuck it.

I reach down and rip off Rayna's shirt. She isn't wearing a bra, though she rarely does. I love catching glimpses of her hardened nipples beneath her shirt, especially when my bones gives zero fucks if anyone sees. There is something unbelievably contagious about her reckless nature.

Fear holds me back, but Rayna has a way of setting me free.

"Changed your mind, huh?" she says as her breasts soak up the sunshine. "I can't be the only one."

She reaches to remove my shirt, and I let her. If we give the train conductor an eyeful before he drags our innards from here to the next station, so be it. She slips off her shoes, and I drop my hands to her jeans, unbuttoning and snatching them down so she can pull them off.

Her hand drops to my back pocket, where she draws my favorite knife from the depths. She smirks at me as she flips open the blade, sticks out her tongue, and drags the strip of silver down the quivering muscle. The skin separates slightly, and dark crimson fills the channel, dripping past her full lower lip when it overflows the wound.

My erection is immediate, and I'm surprised I didn't come in my pants.

She swipes her bleeding tongue over her lips before sucking it back in and looking up at me. I grip her head between two very frustrated hands and inhale every ounce of her lusty, metallic perfume as we kiss. Droplets of blood fall onto my bare chest and warm the skin. They roll down my abdomen and settle against my navel.

With another sadistic smirk, she pulls away and sits on the rail. She spreads her pretty thighs, purses her lips, leans forward, and spits bloody saliva onto her pussy.

"Oh, bones," I growl. She knows my favorite flavor.

She drags her hand through the blood staining her damp skin. "Eat me, Dalton."

I dive to my knees, crawl to her, and send my tongue through her slit. Never mind the gravel digging into my flesh. Her back arches as I devour her. Rocks and metal stab my kneecaps, but I don't care. I couldn't be paid to care as I eat her as if this could be the last thing I taste. And it could be.

Her moans are music to my ears as she breathes them out. She opens her mouth again and lets the bloody line of spit slip down her chest. I only stop eating her to watch the crimson roll over the hardened hill of her nipple and stay there, hovering like some sacred liquid. And it is sacred. I lift my head to capture her flesh and suck the blood from her skin.

My hands fly to the front of my pants, and I rip open my jeans. I tug her off the rail so her ass drops between the tracks, and I wrap her legs around me. I need her. I need her more than I need my next breath as I lick and bite the sweat from her skin.

"Fuck me," she pleads, needing me as much as I need her.

I sit on my knees, spit on her pussy, and pull her into me. She's so fucking warm and wet as I push inside her. Her hands fly up to grip the rusty rail behind her as I lean over and drive my hips forward. Gravel, sticks, and weeds grate against her back, but she doesn't seem to feel any of it. She's too focused on the driving pain and pleasure between her spread thighs.

After a few minutes, I lose myself to the feeling as well. I'm even able to block out the creepy black eyes staring at me from that squirrel's disheveled face. Rayna's body becomes my sole focus, and I worship her in the woods.

"You need to make me come now," she says after a long moan.

I drop my hand between us and rub her swollen clit with my thumb. "Is someone aching to get off already?" I ask through a smirk.

That's when Van Gogh topples over, and I finally feel the vibrations rumbling through the ground.

"Something like that." Rayna rolls her hips and sighs, completely unbothered by the fact that we're about to become a greasy spot on the rails.

"Is that why you brought the fucking squirrel over? Because you knew this was a death sentence and you had to take him with us?"

She smirks, showcasing her beautiful, bloody smile.

"I don't think I can do this, bones."

It's the truth. My cock practically retreats the moment the vibrations register in my knees. She may have zero sense of self-preservation, but personally, I'm kind of enjoying being alive. Mostly.

Sensing my sudden need to flee, Rayna rolls us over and climbs on top of me. She's wrong, though. I won't leave her on these tracks. She'd just start masturbating, determined to fulfill her own prophecy and arrive before the train. If I want both of us to make it out of this alive, I'll need to get her off.

And I need to finish the job, too.

I grip her hips and urge her to ride me harder. I know what she needs in this position, and it's totally up to her to get there. I'm just providing the cock.

"I'm so close," she moans, and I reach up to pinch her nipples.

Her face contorts as the pain zips through her breasts and travels straight to her clenching pussy. Administering the pain helps me as well, causing my dick to jerk inside her as I edge closer to release.

"Fuck, I'm coming. Don't stop." Her movements lose any rhythm as she gives herself carpet burn on my pubic hair. Her pussy grips my dick in an iron fist, and I keep pinching the fuck out of her nipples to keep her there.

If it's a good one, maybe she'll let us both off the tracks, because I really don't think I can get off right now. Not when the train is so close that I can hear it. The whistle wails in the distance, drawing closer with every panting breath we take.

Rayna collapses against my chest. I move to sit up, but she pushes me down again.

"We have to get off the tracks," I say, but when I try to ease her off me, she pushes down on my lap.

"No, I'm not getting off the tracks until *you* get off!" She settles her weight again. "Now fucking fill me!"

"You're insane, bones!"

"And you love it." She rocks her hips, forcing my dick to harden inside her.

I can't fucking help it. This is what she does to me.

I try to forget there's a train coming as I focus on the warm heat squeezing my dick. The vibrations are stronger now. They're so strong, in fact, that my teeth buzz in my skull whenever my head touches the track. But she won't let me go until I've spilled what she's working so hard to pull out of me.

"Hurry, baby," she whispers in my ear. "We're running out of time."

Does she think I don't realize that? Does she think she's *helping?*

Maybe she is, because with the risk of imminent death coming at high speeds toward us, I fill her pussy. My eyes are glued to that distant space on the tracks, but my entire focus is on the place where I empty my soul into hers. The moment I finish, I throw her off me and grab her to haul her off the tracks. The train is pretty much here.

The metal monster breaks through the trees, moving deceptively slow. Again, it's all a trick of the eyes. It's probably going fast enough to dislocate every bone in our bodies. It's close enough to see the conductor's terrified eyes as he spots the tiny naked people stumbling over the ties, and that's too close for comfort.

We stumble to safety, but Rayna and I turn and make the same realization as the train is practically upon us. Raul and Van Gogh still huddle among our clothes on the tracks.

I grab Rayna's waist to stop her from bolting for her beloved friends.

"Let me go!" she screams, and I strain to hold the flailing woman in my grasp.

Her feet fly, and she lands a kick to my nuts. Unable to stay upright, I drop to the ground and lose my grip. Rayna dives onto the tracks and grips her squirrel and beloved butt plug. Then she's lost in a rush of wind and metal.

"Rayna, no!"

I can't take a breath. I'm literally suffocating on nothing more than incomprehensible anguish. I cannot survive without Rayna, and I don't think she got out of the way in time. If she's on the other side of that train, I can't hear her. Even if she's screaming in pain, the roar of the train is too loud for any other sound to filter through.

The train is short, but hours seem to pass as I wait for the graffiti-laden cars to end. When the last one clears my line of sight, I finally breathe a sigh of relief. Rayna is seated on the other side, her squirrel and butt plug clutched firmly to her bare chest.

"I'm okay!" she says with a smile and a wave of her hand.

I rush to her side and check her over, but the only wound I find is the one she made herself on her tongue.

"I said I'm okay," she huffs.

"Don't you *ever* do that again, Rayna. I was about to sit on these tracks until the next train barreled through here and took me with it. There's no life for me without you."

"I'm sorry." She stands on tiptoes and places a soft kiss on my cheek.

"You aren't, though. You'd do it all over again for that fucking squirrel."

"Aw, are you jealous?"

"Jealous?" My eyes widen. "More like incredibly

fucking concerned. You can't throw your life away for a squirrel, bones. And a dead squirrel, at that!"

"You're not as cute as Van Gogh, but . . . I guess I would save you too." She skips over the tracks, grabs our clothes, and tosses them to me.

"Brat," I whisper. "Now get dressed before I have to kill someone for looking at your naked body."

Her eyes light up. "Does that mean we can kill again?"

I sigh and begin dressing. She really is having a hard time with this patience thing.

"Just a few more days until we're in Florida. Let that be enough for now," I say.

She groans and pulls her shirt over her head. "I guess it's nice to have something to look forward to. Like playing with Raul." She wiggles the butt plug toward my face.

Yeah. I'm kind of looking forward to what happens next with Rayna, too. It's always something with her.

# Chapter Three

### Dalton

We take a detour when we hit North Carolina, choosing to cut along the coast so that Van Gogh can smell the sea air. It's really for Rayna, but I play along and pretend we're doing this for our ailing Victorian child. He certainly looks the part as she holds him against the window.

"Are there squirrels on the beach?" she asks as she watches the ocean pass by.

I shrug. "Seagulls would probably be the squirrels of the beach."

"Maybe I can find a taxidermy seagull when we get to Oak Hollow," she says with a beaming smile. She looks down at Van Gogh. "We can get you a cousin."

If the Reddit thread is to be believed, she'll find damn near anything she wants in that town. They've draped every shop, café, and home in death. I wish I could share Rayna's excitement, but I'm thoroughly creeped the fuck out.

She pulls out her phone and types something in

Seconds later, a frown replaces her smile. "Fuck, we'll miss the funeral celebration at this rate."

"Funeral . . . celebration?"

"Yeah, right before Halloween, they display their dead for the year before burying them."

More questions pop into my mind, but I'm too afraid of the answers. Glad our detour will force us to miss out, I take another side road and pull through a strip of souvenir shops. This isn't exactly tourist season for the beach town, but the steady supply of locals must keep them in business.

Rayna sits up taller and focuses on something ahead. I follow her gaze to a man on the side of the road. Unlike the locals, he sticks out. He wears a tattered brown backpack, and road dust covers his clothes. He holds his thumb high in the air, begging for a ride out of here.

"We *have* to stop and pick him up!" Rayna says, her enthusiasm seeping out of every pore.

"We absolutely do *not* have to do that."

"Come on, Dalton. Please!" She adjusts in her seat so that she can face me. "We don't even have to kill him."

"Then what's the point of picking him up?"

She doesn't even need to consider her answer. "We can make him as uncomfortable as possible and see how long it takes him to ask to be let out. Please? For me?"

Her hand slides over my thigh and lands on the crotch of my jeans. Her begging does something to me. It always has. It's how I ended up in my first ever three-way . . . with a corpse. It's how I ended up wearing another man's sausage casing. She begs, and I'm so stupidly in love that I give in.

She's a bad influence.

I pull over and turn to Rayna. "Okay. We can pick him up. But we are not killing him, understood?"

Rayna lets out a joyful squeal and kicks her feet with

the cutest show of excitement I've ever seen. It's as if picking up a dirty man on the side of the road is the greatest gift I could have given her.

I wave to the man, and he approaches the car as I lower the window. "Where you headed?"

As he draws closer, I regret the decision to stop. Despite being grimy from the road, he's incredibly handsome. Hell, the grit might be adding to the allure. When he smiles at me, I want to punch him in the teeth to make them just a little less straight, but then I might slip and cut my fist on that razor-sharp jawline.

He leans down and places his thick forearms on my window, tossing his head to get the quiff of blond hair out of his face. "Florida, but if you're headed south, I'll ride as far as you can take me."

"What a coincidence!" Rayna squeals. "We're headed to Florida too!"

My brain screams to come up with a reason, any reason, to change my mind right now and drive away, but it's too late. He's already opening the back door and settling his pack on the seat. A strange and slightly familiar scent reaches my nose when he sits down and closes the door. I can't quite put my finger on it . . . but I know that odd, leather-like aroma.

"How long have you been hitchhiking?" I ask, trying to beat back the awkward silence with some idle conversation.

"All day." He shuffles around in the back seat.

Rayna turns to see what he's doing, and her eyes go wide. Panic immediately sets in as her mouth falls open. She's never without something to say. I need to keep my eyes on the road, but I'm dying to know what he's revealed that has her so shocked. It better not be his fucking dick. If he so much as looks at Rayna sideways,

I'm breaking my one rule and making the kill my damn self.

Finally, Rayna finds her voice. "Is that a cinnamon? I've never seen one in person."

Cinnamon?

"I see you know your raccoons," the man says.

Raccoon? Did he bring a wild animal into my car?

"And it's a soft mount too? It looks so lifelike." Rayna is practically beaming, and that's when it hits me. The man must have seen her squirrel and pulled out his own bit of taxidermy. But what she says next nearly has me swerving off the road. "Did we just become best friends?"

Did I just pick up the man who will steal the love of my life away from me?

"Why do you carry around a dead raccoon?" I ask, trying to prevent him from answering that question.

"Probably the same reason I carry a dead squirrel around," Rayna quips.

"I just love taxidermy," the man says before sitting back in his seat with the animal draped across his lap. If I lean just right, I can see him in the rearview mirror. And he's still so fucking handsome.

Regret grips my throat in a chokehold. I fucked up. I let the man of Rayna's dreams inside my fucking car. He's the psycho to her pathic, the in to her sane. I'm outside looking in, firmly seated beyond their inner circle as they play a gruesome game of show and tell. Where is Raul when I need him?

If he thinks he'll steal her from me, he's lost it. I'll kill him myself before I let him have her, and I'll burn his stupid raccoon in front of him first.

I firm my grip on the wheel and reel in my sanity. I'm not thinking clearly. Rayna loves me, and she won't hop on the first dick who shares her favorite hobby. Even if he does look a lot like Liam Hemsworth. And even though he's now telling her that he not only owns a taxidermy collection, but he has his own shop.

If we picked up a girl who had a penchant for blood like me, would Rayna feel this intense jealousy I'm feeling now? Either way, killing him will be just the thing to get my mind right.

The next few miles pass in a blur as I try to block out their conversation. Joining in isn't an option, as they're currently discussing the merits of building your own form versus buying a pre-made. I don't know what any of these words mean.

Golden arches appear in the distance as we near the interstate again. McDonald's is Rayna's favorite, and we haven't eaten in hours.

"How about we stop for a bite?" I say to Rayna as I point to the fast-food building coming up on our right.

Rayna shakes her head. "I'm not really hungry right now." She turns back to the stranger. "So, like I was saying, I thought about re-stretching him over a new form, but I think he'd just tear."

"Let me see him," the man says as he holds his hand toward Van Gogh.

I sit a little higher in my seat, knowing she's about to snatch that squirrel back quicker than he can blink. It took a lot of work for her to allow me to touch him, and I know she'd never—

"Be careful with that left ear. It's barely hanging on," she says as she hands the squirrel to the man.

Fuck.

I snatch the wheel and pull into the McDonald's parking lot. Van Gogh flies from Rayna's fingers and smacks into the side of my head, then continues down to the foot-board, where he gets jammed under the brake. Unfortunately, I also press my foot down at the same time, crushing the squirrel's frail body. The resulting crunch might as well have been my own ribcage because now I can't fucking breathe.

Rayna screams as I put the car in park and reach into the shadows to pull up the remains of her most beloved object. At first glance, I'm relieved. He's still in one piece, despite the terrible crunching sound we heard. But then my finger finds the ragged tear running down his side.

"Bones, I'm sorry," I say as I offer him to her.

With tears in her eyes, she pulls the furry creature to her chest and fights back the sobs. I've never seen her look so small and afraid.

"You killed him," she whispers as she studies the strip of separated skin.

Now is not the moment to tell her that he died a long time ago, so I bite my tongue and try to think of something kind to say. That's when Mister Wonderful swoops in.

"Let me see him," he says. He reaches into the front seat once more, and I fight the urge to bite his fingers off. When Rayna places Van Gogh in his waiting palm, my heart sinks again.

I bite back the rage. For her.

After a few moments of tense silence, the man sits forward and places the squirrel in Rayna's lap. "The tear looks worse than it is. You lost a little fur, but I can patch him up if you don't mind making the trip to Oak Hollow."

"Then I guess we're taking you the entire way there," she says.

"Rayna, can I speak to you, please?" I say.

She nods. "Sure."

"Outside the car." I smile sweetly at her. I know I just fucked up, but we are absolutely not taking this strange man the entirety of the journey. In fact, I'm thinking of avoiding that town altogether now.

She sets Van Gogh on the center console and joins me outside the car. Despite being fall, it's uncomfortably warm out, and I begin to sweat almost immediately. Though part of it is probably stress.

"You can't be serious," I whisper when the car door closes. We take a few steps away from the vehicle.

Rayna crosses her arms over her chest and glares at me. "Oh, I'm very serious. I only want the best for Van Gogh, and judging by his racoon, Samuel is the best."

"*Samuel?* You're on a first-name basis with him now?"

"Your shitty driving is the reason my squirrel now has a gash in his side, and he is the key to fixing him. Hell, he might even be able to reattach his dangly ear. Don't you want that for our son, Dalton?"

Her bottom lip quivers as she looks up at me. She's serious.

I sigh and pull her against my chest. "Fine, bones. We'll take him the full way to Oak Hollow."

Now I just have to hope I don't regret this.

# Chapter Four

**Rayna**

We're almost through South Carolina by the time we stop for the night. The leisurely route we'd planned—stopping by various oddity markets and mom-and-pop shops—has evaporated. Dalton seems more than eager to make it to Oak Hollow by the Funeral Celebration now.

I think this has something to do with our new friend. Well, *my* new friend. Dalton looks ready to claw out his eyeballs whenever he opens his mouth to speak.

If he's jealous, he has no reason to be. Despite crushing our baby under the brake pedal, Dalton is still the best thing that's ever happened to me. No one can hold a candle to him, even if they're a six-foot-seven male model who happens to love taxidermy.

We grab our things from the car and head into the motel lobby. Like me, Samuel travels with little more than a backpack. Meanwhile, Dalton struggles to haul his two suitcases from the trunk. A nomadic life hasn't exactly been easy for him.

"Need some help?" Samuel asks him. He steps forward and reaches for the larger bag, but Dalton pulls it closer to his legs and shakes his head. Samuel lifts his hands and smiles. "Suit yourself."

Knowing he absolutely does need help, I grab the smaller bag, and we start inside.

The lobby is dark, and the color brown is the only way to describe it. Walls, carpet, desk, chairs—everything is some shade of diarrhea brown. Stale cigarette smoke clings to everything in sight, despite the large sign on the lobby desk stating that ciggies are off-limits. When the older woman behind the desk smiles, I can easily figure out who the culprit is by looking at her yellow-stained smile.

"Oh, are we having a fun little party tonight?" she says with a wiggle of her shoulders. Her smile falls when she looks at Samuel. "Sorry, honey. No pets."

"Not even dead ones?" He wiggles the raccoon, and the woman realizes her mistake.

"Goodness, why?" she asks as her hand flies to her chest.

My hand flies to my chest, and I look at her with a straight face as I say, "Goodness, why *not*?"

The woman purses her lips and clears her throat before pulling her chair a bit closer to the desk and banging on the noisy keyboard. "What sort of room do you need? Single? Double?"

"Two rooms, please," Dalton says, and he even holds up his fingers to make sure she gets the memo. When he tries to pay with cash, however, things go a bit south.

"We require a credit card in case our patrons decide to trash our rooms. An insurance policy, if you will." She glances around the dark space. "It isn't exactly cheap to replace things which have been ruined by rowdy guests."

Could have fooled me. You could easily replace any of this shit with something you'd find at a local flea market. Bonus points if the items wear a cloak of cigarette smoke.

"We don't carry a card," I say. "Perhaps we could throw a little on top as an insurance policy?"

She places her hand to her chest again, this time mocking me the way I mocked her. "I don't think so, sweetie."

Before I can launch myself over the lip of the desk and rip out her eyeballs, Samuel steps forward and pushes a credit card across the sticky wooden surface. The woman snatches up the rectangle of plastic, giving Dalton and me no room to argue. She's swiped it and printed two receipts faster than we can take our next breath.

On the way outside, Dalton tries to give Samuel the cash, but Samuel shrugs him off.

"You guys are hauling me across the country. The least I can do is spot you for the night."

Dalton opens his mouth to argue, but I grab his arm and pull him through the lobby door and into the chill fall air. If he wants to be jealous, that's fine, but I draw the line at sabotaging a chance to save some cash. He needs to keep his pride to himself.

We part ways with Samuel as we reach the rusty stairs on the side of the building. He gives us a smile and heads down the row toward his lower-level room, and we head up the dangerous tetanus steps. Dalton doesn't return Samuel's smile, but I do. It's just good manners.

The air in the motel room is stale, but at least it doesn't smell like the desk lady's lair. I sit on the edge of the bed. I'm disappointed when it's like sitting on a wooden box instead of a cloud. Disappointed, but not surprised. We don't exactly have the funds to stay at the Hilton.

Van Gogh will stay in my bag for the night. I hate the thought of him in that dark space, all cooped up without any fresh air, but I'm scared to death the rip in his side might spread. Plus, seeing that gash makes me uncomfortable. It was an accident, so I'm not angry with Dalton, but it still makes me sick.

"Nice to finally be alone," Dalton says as he drops the bag on the floor and flops beside me on the bed. He rolls onto his side and traces the floral print on the comforter with his extended finger. "You feeling kind of tired, or . . . ?"

I grab his hand and place it on my thigh. "I'm tired, but I could use a little stress relief to help take the edge off of today."

"Mmm, say less." Dalton inches closer and nips my inner thigh. "You wanna play with Raul? He didn't get his moment, thanks to the train."

My heart soars when he mentions one of my newest treasures. Dalton is always game to do what I want, but sometimes he requires a little coaxing. I like it best when he willingly throws my kinks into the mix.

I scramble off the side of the bed and pull Raul from my bag. After placing him on the side table so that his little glass eyes can watch my man work my body, I step into Dalton. He sits on the edge of the mattress with his hands between his knees. His fingertips brush my shirt hem, gripping that thin edge and raising it until his breath whispers over my bare breasts. He dips lower, nipping my stomach and lashing my skin with his tongue.

"What are you thinking about?" I whisper.

"That woman in the front office," he growls against my skin.

Instead of feeling jealous, I moan and run my fingers through his hair, pulling him closer. Because he isn't thinking about fucking that woman. He's thinking about killing her.

"How would you do it?" I push his head lower, and he drags his warm tongue over my hip bone before lowering my shorts.

He smirks against my skin, then admires my pussy before putting a voice to his imagined fantasy. As he talks, he dips his fingers into my warmth, teasing my clit and making everything slippery with desire.

"First and foremost, I'd make sure Van Gogh is there to witness it, just for her sideways remark," he says. "Then I'd tie her to the chair and break open a vein. Not enough to kill her, mind you. Just enough to make everything red and spread a little panic through her soul."

I imagine her blood, how it would make everything so slippery. "Keep going," I beg.

His fingers pick up speed, running faster, harder circles over that sensitive place. "Once she's good and terrified, I'll bring you into the room. I'll strip you down, bend you over, and push Raul into your tight little asshole, all while she watches."

"Fuck yes." I roll my hips, chasing the pleasure he tempts me with. "Make me come."

"I'll make you—"

A knock at the door silences us. We freeze and stare at the window to the right of it, wondering who in their right mind would bother us when it's nearly midnight. Dalton looks at my clothes on the floor, but there's no time to dress. The knock comes again, and it's a little louder this time.

"The knife," he whispers, and I nod and pull my hunting knife from my pack before moving to the other side of the bed and dropping behind it, leaving only my face exposed. If I have to charge someone naked, fine, but they don't get to look at my goodies for free unless I want them to. And whoever this is doesn't have that privilege.

Dalton creeps to the door and peers through the peephole. His shoulders droop immediately.

"Who is it?" I whisper.

He sighs and steps away from the door. "Put your clothes on. It's your little *friend*."

I like Samuel, but his timing is not the best. I'll give Dalton that much. Still, it's not like we can't politely shoo him away. We don't have to be dicks to him.

After I pull on my clothes, Dalton opens the door. Samuel offers a friendly smile, complete with a wave. Dalton returns neither gesture.

"Hope I wasn't interrupting anything," he says with a shake of the bottle in his hands. "Figured I'd see if you guys wanted to share a drink. It's just some cheap whiskey I picked up on my travels, but it's good enough for a nightcap."

"I think we're good for the night, thanks." Dalton tries to close the door, but I bolt forward and wrench it open.

Forcing a smile, I motion him into our room. "Sorry, he's a bit tired. He gets rude when he hasn't had a nap." I pin Dalton with a glare as I lead Samuel into our accommodations.

Look, I get it. He wants to be alone with me, and I want that as well, but we're talking about the surgeon who will repair my ailing baby. We need to play nice and get on his good side, especially if we hope to get this done at a price we can afford: free.

"If you guys need to go to bed—"

"Nonsense," I say, waving off Samuel's comment.

Dalton dies a little inside, but he stomps over to the bed and flops down without any other argument. This is really throwing a stick into his spokes, but we're almost to Florida. Once Samuel patches up Van Gogh, things can go back to normal. Until then, I'll just have to continue navigating this very tense situation.

# Chapter Five

### Dalton

I hate everything about him, from his perfect appearance to his smooth voice. He fucking sucks, and now he can add cock-blocking to his list of transgressions. Thankfully, the whiskey bottle is nearly empty now. I've been chugging the shit to hurry this little shindig along.

While Rayna and Mr. Perfect have been poring over her small taxidermy collection, I've been sitting on the edge of the bed and stewing. A small part of my soul knows that I'm being silly, that Rayna is loyal and I have nothing to fear. A larger part of my soul wants nothing more than to rid the world of this man, if for no other reason than he's looked at my bones a little too long. He smiles at her a little too brightly.

When two o'clock rolls around and the bottle is well and truly empty, he finally stands and stretches. "Guess I'd best let you two get some sleep if we want to make up some miles tomorrow. I'm happy to take turns driving if you ever need a break."

First he wants to steal my woman, and now he wants to drive my car? I don't fucking think so.

"Thanks, I'll keep that in mind." I hurry behind him to the door so that he can't change his mind and make himself comfortable again. I close the door behind him as he turns to say goodnight. "Have a nice sleep. Or die. Either one."

"Dalton," Rayna whispers. "He might've heard you!"

I shrug. The fucks are buried in my black heart, and I can't give them.

The poor girl pulls me into her and tries to soothe me by rubbing my dick outside my pants, but I'm too pissed off to get hard now. I can't compete with him, and it's only a matter of time before Rayna realizes he's the better option for her. That realization is a bit of a buzzkill.

But then I remember that I can give her something he'll never be able to. I can give her murder. I can assist her in exploring every fantasy she could possibly conjure.

With a drunken leer, I stalk toward my prey. She stumbles backward with a giggle, her delicate fingers held to her chest as she sits on the edge of the mattress. She falls in line without any effort, and we're right back to the game we were playing before we were so rudely interrupted.

I lean over her on the bed and trail kisses from her neck to her navel. The memory of Samuel fades with every inch I draw closer to her warmth. By the time her soft thighs rub against my cheeks, I'm no longer frustrated. I'm focused solely on this woman and what she does to me.

And what I can do to her.

"Flip onto your stomach and lower your shorts," I command.

Rayna nibbles her lip and does as she's told. I love how

flexible she is, able to slot into the role of master or dog at will. Right now, she's beholden to my pleasure, ready to lap up whatever I spill at her feet.

She lowers her shorts, exposing her perfect ass to me. I stroke my cock through the deep seam, depositing some pre-cum at her back entrance to act as lube. After adding a little spit to the mixture, I rub my thumb through the slippery sensation and revel in the way her back arches.

Then I reach for Raul.

I've put things in Rayna's butt before, so this is nothing new, but being forced to stare into the face of something's death mask is uncharted territory. Aside from the dead *people*, of course. When put up against everything else we've done, it doesn't seem that different, yet I'm struggling as I press the plug against her asshole. She doesn't seem bothered, however. A moan rolls past her parted lips, followed by a satisfied sigh.

"Fuck, that is going to feel so good," she breathes. "I'm ready."

With a little pressure, the plug slides past the tight ring of muscles, and Raul is firmly seated in place. I give his head a slight twist to properly orient his face, and Rayna's toes curl.

"Yeah, fuck with it when it's inside me," she says. "That feels so good."

I line up behind her and press my cock against her entrance. She doesn't give me time to ease into her. Instead, she rocks back and forces my dick fully inside her. My head tips back as I suck air through my teeth and grip her hips.

"Didn't say I was ready, bones."

She smirks at me over her shoulder. "You'll never be fully ready for me."

She's not wrong about that. This little vixen is always

full of surprises, which is what keeps me coming back for more. I'll never be ready for her, but I'm always ready for the next shock she'll drop on my dick.

As I push forward, Raul's smile brushes against my pelvis, and I try to mentally distance myself from the animal. That isn't hard to do when I raise my gaze just a bit and focus on the back of Rayna's head. Her dark hair glistens in the low light, the strands falling haphazardly over her pale shoulder. I run my hand through the wild tresses and pull them tight against her scalp.

Something about gripping her hair this way sends her into a state of relaxation I could never hope to experience. Her muscles dissolve, and the dip in her back drives lower. Her eyes roll in her head as she looks at the ceiling and sees nothing.

"I can't hold back anymore," Rayna says, and with a stunning cry, she comes on my cock.

Rayna convulses beneath me, and I'm in heaven. This is why I need her. She can please me in ways no other woman can. As I clutch her against my body and fill her with all that I am, I can't lose her.

"I love you, bones," I whisper into the air.

She turns her head and smiles at me. "I love you too."

That's when I know that I have to make this official in the most final way. When we reach Oak Hollow, I'm going to propose to Rayna.

# Chapter Six

**Rayna**

The start to the day was a bit later than we wanted, but it couldn't be helped. After the incredible butt-plug sex, we slept like the dead. If Samuel hadn't started banging on the door at ten in the morning, we'd have missed our checkout time. Thankfully, we made it, and after driving all day, we've finally crossed into Florida.

We turn onto a long stretch of dark road. The car bumps along pavement that buckled years ago and has now fallen further into disrepair. Despite the welcoming website that talks about the city's rich history, it would appear they don't exactly welcome tourism. Not unless you plan to parachute in, I guess.

I sit in the passenger seat, clutching Van Gogh to my chest as the town sign comes into view. Oak Hollow. As soon as we pass the sign, the road smooths out like butter.

Turning in my seat, I look at Samuel. "What's up with

the road? Why is it so shitty out that way, then nice once you reach town?"

"Everything has kind of . . . shifted. A fire has burned under this land for the last fifty years and will probably burn long past our deaths."

"Beneath us?" I ask.

"All the coal mines."

Okay, I'm *very* invested in this creepy town now. A fire that burns beneath it? That's the most metal thing I've ever heard of. My mind races with questions. Is the ground hotter? Is there smoke? Will we die from gases or something?

We pass through the town's main street. It looks like something out of a movie, with quaint shop signs catching the moon's glow. To look at this place without knowing what it is, you'd never suspect these people are death obsessed. But when you look a bit closer, it's more than apparent.

"Is that a wind chime made of bones?" I ask as we drive past a massive house with a gorgeous wraparound porch.

"It is. My father made that for my mother as a wedding gift. The two spines belonged to thieves in a remote village in the Amazon. Father worked with the tribe, taking the pieces of the dead the tribe deemed unclean. We aren't that superstitious."

"That was your house?" My eyes can't possibly get any wider. I never expected the dirty man we plucked from the side of the road would also live in a southern mansion.

Samuel nods. "Well, it's my father's house. He's the former mayor of Oak Hollow. My brother holds that title now, along with funeral-director-slash-coroner. Mayor, coroner, funeral director—the three go hand in hand here."

As we near the city's center, the road opens up, and

bright lights twirl in the distance. In a green courtyard stands a carousel, but as the car creeps closer, I can see that the horses aren't the fabricated versions I'm used to. They're covered in fur, frozen in various death poses, and they're undoubtedly the real deal—functional taxidermy.

"Can people ride that, or is it an art installment?" I ask.

Samuel's smile broadens. "Of course you can ride it. It's open every day from ten to six, but they keep it open a little later during the celebration. The kids really get a kick out of it."

"Kids?" Dalton blurts. "You people raise children around this?"

I swat his thigh to shut him up, because how fucking rude. "Why wouldn't they raise kids here? Nothing wrong with a little death. Don't be a judgmental asshole like that lady at the motel."

"Speaking of her, I felt a bit bad about leaving without dropping off our keys. Hopefully that doesn't come back to bite me in the ass. If I see a security fee on my card, I'm coming after you two." Samuel lets out a laugh and motions for me to turn right on the next street.

The headlights catch on houses that spread further and further apart. Eventually, we're driving through the countryside as we cut a path up a small mountain about three miles outside of the town proper. The road eventually becomes a dirt track that dead-ends at a small wooden house.

Samuel gathers his things and opens the back door to exit the car. He pauses. "I don't live as lavishly as my father, but you two are welcome to stay the night. The Oak Hollow Inn doesn't staff the desk past ten, so you're out of luck there. I have a spare bedroom, so you'd have privacy."

Before Dalton can say no, I smile and accept his offer.

"We'd appreciate it. Maybe tomorrow you could take a closer look at Van Gogh?"

"It might take a few days, but I'll comp your room at the Inn while you're stuck waiting."

Dalton scoffs, and I swat his arm.

"That's fine," I say. "Is the hole in his side really that bad, though?"

Samuel runs his hand through his hair and shakes his head. "No, it's not that. The hole won't take more than a few minutes to patch, but if you want him cleaned up and improved, he'll need more time."

I look down at Van Gogh. He might be a little crusty around the edges, but do I really want to change him? His raggedy appearance is part of his charm, after all.

"Maybe just fix the ear and the hole in his side. I don't want him to be too different." I lick my lips and hand him to Samuel.

With the squirrel clutched in one hand and his pack slung over his other shoulder, he exits the car, and we follow him to the wooden porch. Another strange wind chime hangs from the railing, though this one appears to be made from various bacula. Aged boards creak underfoot as we ascend the steps, and insects scream from the darkness.

"Creepy," I whisper.

Samuel turns to me and smiles. "I know. Isn't it glorious?"

I smile and turn to Dalton, hoping to see some excitement on his face, but he still seems to be processing the fact that we'll be staying the night at Samuel's house. I'll just have to set his mind at ease once we're behind closed doors.

It's really too bad those closed doors appear to be behind basement stairs, as that's where Samuel is currently leading us. Dalton files behind him on the narrow staircase, and I tuck in close behind Dalton. Eerie spaces don't normally make me feel so uncomfortable, but something about this feels very . . . off.

A large metal door waits at the bottom of the stairs. Samuel pushes it open, but it doesn't appear to lock, so that's encouraging. At least we can't get locked in.

But that also means we can't lock anything out.

"The spare room is in the basement?" I ask. "I figured you would keep your shop down here."

"The shop is through the woods. It's larger than the house, actually. I wanted a detached workspace to avoid all the chemicals and such. Too much exposure is bad for the brain, you know." He throws me a sly smile.

Once he's through the doorway, he flicks a switch to the right, and dim overhead lights give us the gift of sight. The bulbs cast a yellow glow on everything, or maybe that's just from the age of the decor.

A low wooden bed hugs the far wall, the foot huddled near the rustic stonework fireplace. Some sort of large brown fur covers the bed—probably buffalo, judging by the pile. Elk, deer, and other antlered ungulates line the walls. If I weren't fighting off a bad vibe, I'd be in heaven.

"Did you . . . kill all of these animals yourself?" Dalton asks as he peers at the death masks. "If so, you're quite the hunter."

Samuel tips back his head with a laugh as he opens a wardrobe, revealing a television. "No, I don't kill animals for sport. The trophies were taken by my brother. He enjoys the killing. I enjoy the art of preservation." He tosses a black remote onto the bed, then heads for the door. "I have local channels, but not much else. The bathroom's through that door"—he nods at a narrow doorway near the back of the room—"and I'll prepare breakfast around nine. If that isn't early enough for you, you're welcome to head to the inn, so long as it's after seven."

"Nine is fine," I say.

Samuel offers a final smile, then leaves us alone in the basement. I had originally planned to relieve Dalton's worries, but now I'm starting to have some worries of my own.

I sit on the edge of the bed and run my hand along the rough fur. "Dalton," I whisper, "I'm not so sure about this."

Dalton's hands drop to his sides, and he stares at me. "Now, bones? *Now* you aren't so sure about this? Once we're in the killer's basement, deep in the fucking woods? *Now* you're *concerned?*"

"Well . . . yes. Better late than never, though."

He sighs and drops beside me on the bed. "Tomorrow, we get Van Gogh, injured or not, and we leave. Deal?"

I nibble my lip and nod. It's probably for the best. Something really doesn't sit right about this place, and I don't want to find out why.

# Chapter Seven

### Rayna

The alarm blares at nine, pulling Dalton and me from a restless sleep. To be fair, I don't know if Dalton slept at all. Each time I woke and turned to look at him, he was staring at the multitude of dead things in the room. At least he knows what's bothering him. I still can't put my finger on what's making *me* so uneasy.

It's just a feeling. An intuition. And I should listen to it.

A thick perfume wafts beneath the door as I blink back the little bit of sleep I found overnight. The aroma of bacon, eggs, and rising dough shifts my stomach from a nervous twist to a roiling growl.

"How'd you sleep?" I ask Dalton.

"Sleep? What is this foreign concept?" he growls as he sits up and rubs his eyes. "Doesn't matter. We'll eat some breakfast to be polite, and then we'll grab the squirrel and put this place behind us. We can get him fixed up some-where a little less creepy."

"It's really saying something that this place is making both of us uncomfortable," I say with a shiver.

We rise from bed, but we don't bother dressing. We slept fully clothed. In the backs of our minds, I think we both recognized the very real possibility that we would need to run. This place just exudes that ominous feeling.

When we reach the door, I fully expect to find the damn thing locked, but we breathe a collective sigh of relief as it groans open with the slightest tug. Dalton leads the way as we climb the stairs and step into the kitchen.

The creepy feeling recedes as sunshine streams through the gauzy yellow curtains. Light catches on a crystal vase in the window and casts a rainbow burst along the sill. A smiling taxidermy racoon holds a wine bottle in a miniature canoe on the counter. It's all very quaint. Peaceful. Almost kitschy.

"Morning, you two," Samuel says from the stove. His hulking form hovers over a pan of scrambled eggs, his forearms flexing as he stirs the mixture. "Breakfast is almost ready, and then you two can head into town to grab a room for the night. I've already spoken with the innkeeper, so she's expecting you."

Dalton takes a seat at the small table near a window. "We appreciate it, Sam, but we talked about it, and I think it's best we head on from here."

"Samuel," he says without dropping his smile, and I don't miss the hidden right hook.

Neither does Dalton. His head rears back slightly, and he clears his throat. "My apologies, Samuel. But as I said, we have to keep moving."

"Hate to hear it, but I understand. I sewed up the squirrel's side already, but he's unable to be moved for a few days. I can always ship him to—"

"No!" I scream. My legs nearly give out, so I sit in a chair beside Dalton before I collapse. "I mean, I can't be away from him. And thinking about him in a tiny box, getting squished or forgotten . . ."

Dalton reaches over and places his hand on mine, then looks at Samuel. "Couldn't you tell us how to properly handle him? I mean, he isn't exactly in great shape, so I don't see how we could fuck him up much more than he already is."

"That's where you're wrong." Samuel shovels the eggs onto the plates lining the counter, followed by a few strips of bacon, fluffy biscuits, and a pat of butter. He slides the plates onto the table, then takes a seat beside Dalton. "If he isn't kept in the proper conditions as the skin sets, he could end up too brittle. That crack in his side will be a splinter compared to the devastation of his entire hide crumbling to dust."

"D-dust? I need water." I lick my lips, but my mouth is a desert.

Dalton gives me a glare, probably internally panicking at the possibility that I'll change my mind and say we'll stay. He's right to panic.

"Well . . . maybe we can stick around for forty-eight hours, but then we really—"

My loving boyfriend kicks me beneath the table. I get it. I do. But we're talking about Van Gogh.

"Forty-eight hours should be just enough time for the hide to set." Samuel's smile returns as he slathers butter onto his biscuit. "Besides, we'll be starting the Funeral Cele-bration tomorrow, and you wouldn't want to miss that."

Meanwhile, Dalton looks like he's about to burst into flames.

I lean over my plate and try to eat. The food is delicious,

but I can't enjoy any of it. I can't shake the feeling that we're being held hostage, that Samuel is dangling my squirrel above my head. And I still can't figure out why . . .

When I finally push my plate away, Dalton stands from the table. He hasn't even touched his food. "I guess we'll head down to the inn now," he says with a forced smile. At least he's trying, I guess. "Thanks for the hospitality."

"Of course." Samuel dabs his full lips with a napkin and then rises to shake Dalton's hand. "I'll see you again, of course. I have your squirrel, don't forget."

"No, we haven't forgotten." Dalton shakes his hand—maybe a bit too aggressively.

We walk to the door with Samuel on our heels, but he doesn't pass the threshold. As we nervously exit at a brisk walk, he just leans against the door and watches us.

He no longer smiles, however.

"Okay, I'm officially creeped the fuck out," I say as soon as I close the car door.

Dalton shoves the keys into the ignition, cranks the car, and begins backing out. "Then please explain why you agreed to remain in this shithole for two more days."

"Van Gogh—"

The car jerks to a stop at the end of the long driveway, and Dalton throws the shifter into park. "Rayna, I love you. I love every part of you, even the weird parts that are fucking scary. But that squirrel is going to get us *killed!*"

I have no argument, so I just sink into my seat and pout. Because he's right. If it weren't for my ridiculous attachment to an inanimate object, we could just leave.

"I'm sorry," I whisper.

Dalton sighs and puts the car in drive again. Once we're on the road, he places his hand on my thigh and gives it a squeeze. "I know he's important to you. I'm the one who's sorry. It's just . . . this place is wrong."

"It's not as if we can't protect ourselves. I mean, remember who we are. We're the Halloween Harvesters! We can't let the assholes out-creep us."

A house drifts by on our right. I stare at it as we pass, noting how abandoned it feels. The lawn is maintained, and a car sits in the driveway, but the property exudes a feeling of forgottenness.

"It feels almost like a ghost town, doesn't it?" I say.

Dalton shivers. "I'm hoping that was just because we drove through at night, when everything was closed up for the evening. Maybe things will seem a little more lively in the daytime. Hell, maybe the next two days won't even be that bad."

I nod and try to swallow that uneasy feeling as we pass another eerie house. Once again, it looks lived in and cared for, but it's almost like a show home. A set dressing.

But as we come into town, the uneasy feeling grows until it can't be swallowed. It crawls up my throat and begs to be released in a shout. A warning. Something isn't right, and for once, it's not because of us.

The town appears, and we drive along the main street that cuts past the carousel. That's when I finally see the first townsperson. An old woman sits in a metal folding chair at the entrance to the merry-go-round. Her jaw moves as she chews something, her sagging jowls wiggling with every mastication. A baggy brown sweater swallows her torso, and she clutches a taxidermy fox to her chest.

"Want to stop and take a spin?" Dalton asks. He's joking, but I nod my head. "What? Bones, you can't be serious."

"I am. If we're stuck here, we might as well explore."

With a groan, he pulls into the parking lot. "You owe me so big for this."

"Noted."

As we climb out of the car, I feel almost naked without Van Gogh. This is the sort of adventure he would have loved. It's also unfortunate that I've finally found people who love dead things as much as I do, yet they creep me out as much as they excite me. Is this how I make others feel?

I ask Dalton this question as we approach the fence surrounding the carousel. He stops, thinks it over, then turns to me.

"Yes, that's exactly how you make me feel. You excite me, but you scare the living shit out of me too."

I roll my eyes. "Noted."

"Oh, look! We have visitors, Mr. Fox!" The woman points the fox's head toward us so that he can "see" us. "Have you come to ride the Magic-Go-Round?"

"No, we're just taking a walk for our health," Dalton mutters, and I ram my elbow into his side.

"Yes," I say to the woman. "May we take a turn on your beautiful carousel?"

She titters to herself—or maybe to Mr. Fox—before struggling to stand. She sets the fox on the worn metal chair and hobbles to the horses skewered through their shoulders by metal poles. Once she's pulled herself onto the platform, she motions for us to join her.

"Just give me a moment to find the right horses for you, dear," she says as she walks through the animals.

I run my hand along the back of what was once a glorious bay. Its head pulls inward as its legs stretch in a wild run. None of the horses wear a saddle, and they look so lifelike that it feels like I'm standing in a wild herd as God freezes time.

"I'm fine with this one," I say as I pat the large bay's stiff muzzle.

The old woman looks back at me, but her smile shifts to shock and dread. "Goodness, come away from that horse! He's a real devil, that one. Much too wild for a young lady. I know just the horse for you, and I've worked the stables all my life, so I would be the one to know."

I glance at Dalton. His eyes are wide, and his jaw hangs open, but he manages to shake his head in warning. *Just play along,* that look says.

So we do. We follow the woman through the horses as she tells us their names and their temperaments, and for the first time in my life, I'm able to see myself through someone else's eyes. I am fucking weird.

"This one will do for you. Her name is Belle, and she's a good-minded animal." The woman pats a palomino whose death pose is just to stand there for eternity and look bored. She turns to the animal beside it and motions for Dalton to climb aboard. "This is my mule, Dusty. If he gives you any trouble and doesn't want to move, just give him a little squeeze and he'll make tracks." She pats the creature's ass and laughs.

We climb aboard our steeds as the woman teeters and totters to the controls in the machinery's center. Seconds later, organ music springs to life, and the carousel begins to turn. The animals don't rise and fall as we begin our first revolution, but the speed increase is enough to give me a thrill. By the third turn, I'm clutching Belle's mane as if my life depends on it.

"Jesus fuck!" Dalton screams. "You'd think this would be less dangerous than actual horseback riding!"

The woman cackles from inside the stationary center, and the music grows louder. Or maybe it just seems to grow louder because I'm already overstimulated. Just when I'm about to scream and throw myself from the ride, a calming touch lands on my thigh.

"How do I let you talk me into these messes?" Dalton pleads, but his touch is all warmth and security. He won't let me run, but he won't let me fall, either.

I close my eyes and press my forehead to the post running through the horse's withers. After a few more agonizing moments of sheer hell, the ride finally slows to a stop. The woman hobbles over and helps us down, and I've never been more grateful to step away from a dead animal in all my life.

"Children ride this thing?" I ask as we stagger off the platform.

"Oh, they did. They used to ride it all the time."

"Used to?" Dalton asks.

But the woman has already stumbled off the platform and wandered back to her chair. It appears she's finished talking to us. She plucks up her fox, then sits and strokes its fur as she mumbles something to it.

"Well, this was fun," I say. We gather ourselves as the spinning feeling recedes, and once we can see straight, we head toward the woman. "Could you at least tell us where we can find the inn?"

She doesn't answer me with words. No, that would be too normal. Instead, she raises a gnarled finger and points to a road running through shadows. Oak trees guard both sides of the pavement like sentries.

"Should have figured it would be *that* road," Dalton mutters.

I grab his hand and head for the car. Maybe we should make a little detour and destress before heading to our next objective.

Once we're finally back in the safety of our vehicle, with locked doors and windows rolled up, I pull out our activity list and start looking through it. Dalton does a double take when he notices.

"You can't be serious. Now isn't the time for fun and games, bones. We are the creepiest people I know, so if *we* are getting creeped out, I think it's time to leave. I'll spend the rest of my life making this up to you, but we have got to get out of this town."

He's right. But I can't leave Van Gogh.

"Forty-eight hours, Dalton. After that, I promise we'll leave."

He sighs and starts the car, and off to the inn we go.

# Chapter Eight

## Dalton

Despite the inauspicious path we took to get here, the inn is the most cheerful looking building I've seen in this town. The oak trees eventually opened up, allowing some fall sunshine to peek through the clouds and shine on the antiquated Victorian-style house. The gingerbread eaves give the building a fairytale quality that is very at odds with literally everything else we've seen in Oak Hollow.

I put the car in park, and our feet crunch through fresh gravel as we make our way to the front porch. A wind chime sings from above the railing, but this one isn't made of bone. It's your typical metal-tube contraption. The sound is much less unsettling.

A tiny bell trills as we open the front door and step inside. An older woman seated at a large wooden desk pops her head up and smiles as we enter. After pushing her glasses up her thin nose, she plucks up a pen and pulls a ledger from a drawer. Her gray ponytail barely wiggles as she sits back in her seat.

"How many guests should we set the table for?" she asks with a giggle.

Rayna looks to me for an answer. Great.

"Just the two of us, but we were looking for a room, not lunch."

The woman nods, then replaces the ledger in the drawer before pulling out a different one. When she speaks again, her voice has changed. Instead of light and airy, she sounds tired, as if every one of her years has finally caught up to her at this very moment.

"Are the two of you married? If not, you can't have a room with only one bed. You have to sleep in separate beds." She says this without looking at either of us. Her entire focus remains on the ledger as she flips pages and exudes condescension. "I have one room with two beds. For two nights, your total will be—"

"Total? Oh, our friend said the room would be comped," Rayna blurts, and my stomach twists when she calls Samuel our friend.

The woman clears her throat. "Yes, well, that's why it's best to let people finish speaking, hmm? Your total will be nothing, as your room has been covered by the town's mayor."

"Rude," Rayna mutters under her breath.

I step forward before she launches herself over the desk. "We appreciate the hospitality, but could we see the room first? We won't be staying in a basement, will we?"

"Basement?" The woman screws up her nose as she rounds the desk and grabs a key from the holder on the wall. "Why on earth would we put you in the basement? That's where we house the bodies."

"Excuse me, did you just say bodies?" My legs keep following her, even though my brain says to run for the door.

She starts up the stairs, and Rayna has to push me to keep me moving. "Yes, the bodies of our dead. The inn is also the funeral home and morgue, you see. And the most popular restaurant in town, thanks to our chef."

"You have a personal chef?" Rayna asks.

The woman stops at the top of the stairs and turns to face us with a smile. When she speaks, she uses a French accent this time. "You are, how do you say, looking at her, no?" With a laugh, she turns and leads us to a door.

I fight the urge to look back at Rayna and mouth, *What the actual fuck is happening?* Because this just gets odder by the second. At least this woman doesn't put me at risk of losing the love of my life. I can almost handle the creep factor as long as Samuel isn't in our vicinity.

When the door swings wide, we step into a bedroom and glimpse two child-sized beds. They cower against the far walls like terrified rabbits, and I don't know how we're expected to sleep on crib mattresses. At least the room is clean, I guess.

Rayna drops her backpack on the bed closest to the door. She runs her hands down her jean-clad thighs and peers at the room as if she's stepped into her own version of hell. It's a bit too white, clean, and clinical. The lacey curtains and gold-trimmed furniture don't help, either.

The older woman's voice changes again, this time shifting to that sweet voice we first heard. "If you aren't joining us for our lunch service, we do hope you'll make it to dinner. It's served promptly at six p.m. in the dining room on the first floor. Tonight's menu is meatloaf with a bird's nest."

With that, she turns and leaves.

"Okay, what the fuck is a bird's nest?" Rayna whispers once the woman's footsteps recede down the hallway.

"I'm more concerned with how the fuck we're supposed to sleep on these beds. Rayna . . . this is doll furniture."

A sly smirk slides across her beautiful face. "Who said anything about sleeping? I thought maybe we could partake in a little fun this evening."

"As tempting as that is, I think it's best we keep our wits about us. Something is off about this place. Who keeps the morgue at the inn, bones?" I shake my head. "I have a bad feeling about this."

She pokes out her lower lip and flops back on the bed. "You mean to tell me you can resist this? *All* of this?" Her fingers raise the hem of her shirt, giving me a perfect view as she slides her hand beneath her waistband with a moan. "Fuck, the fear almost makes it better."

Tearing my eyes away from her, I kneel at the side of the bed and unzip my luggage. "I don't doubt that, but we'll have plenty of time for getting each other off once we're out of this town. Until then, we have to stay focused."

Rayna's nails tickle my scalp before she grabs my hair and tugs my mouth toward her pussy. "Fucking taste me. You know you want to."

I press my lips to the crotch of her jeans and blow warm breath against her. She's right. I want to taste her. I want to devour her and drink every drop of her pleasure straight from the source. Especially when she moans like that and grinds against my face.

But it isn't wise.

"We could check off another tick on the adventure list, you know," she whispers as I nibble her from outside her jeans. "Remember the—"

"I remember."

"The morgue is just downstairs . . ."

When I agreed to an orgy among a body pile, I thought that it would be bodies of our own making. Victims of this year's harvest. The final crescendo of passion after a night of symphonic murder. To utilize bodies of people who didn't die by our hands feels kind of gross. Inauthentic.

"I don't know, bones. I really think we should keep our heads on a swivel. As much as I want you to sit on me and rotate, this place is fucking dangerous."

Rayna sits up with a shrug, but I know that mischievous glint in her eyes. "Fine. If you don't want to check out the morgue, have fun sitting on this bed. I'm going down there."

As she stands and leaves the room, I don't argue. It would be pointless. Instead, I simply stand and follow her as she creeps down the hallway.

"There may not be enough bodies for this," I whisper. "It's a small town. How many dead people can they have down there?"

"Shh!" Rayna pins me with a glare, and I close my mouth. She motions through the stair railing, and I peer over the side. Down below, the older woman sits at her desk, scrawling something into a ledger.

"Any idea how we'll sneak past her?" I ask. "We don't even know where the morgue is."

Rayna points again, and I see a placard beside a door that reads MORGUE. Touche.

Still, we'll be forced to sneak past that desk to reach it.

"We'll need some sort of distraction," Rayna whispers.

"Oh, is that all? Well, let me just pull this distraction machine out of my pocket, and—"

I'm silenced by the bell tinkling above the front door as it swings open. Rayna and I sink further into the shadows so that the guest doesn't see us, but I saw enough of that sharp jaw to know that it was Samuel. Seconds later, their voices filter up to us.

"Are they in their room?" Samuel asks.

The woman scoffs, using her hotel-lobby-desk-clerk voice when she speaks this time. "You know how I feel about unwed couples rooming together. Couldn't you have found a single woman instead of one who was already attached? What if this goes as poorly as the last one?"

Rayna and I look at each other.

"It won't," Samuel says. Boots scuff on the floor, and then he continues. "This one's right. She has a pet squirrel she carries around, and she'll fit right into the family. I'm sure of it. She already met Granny at the magic-go-round."

"And what of the man?"

"We needed a sacrifice, didn't we? The busted roads keep out the investigators, but they keep out the tourists as well. I can't keep pulling from the local town, Mama. You know it's not safe anymore."

*Sacrifice?* I mouth to Rayna.

She blinks at me, her eyes growing wider.

"They'll take off the moment they get a wild hair," the woman says. "They're already jumpy."

"I've got her squirrel. I lied and said he needed time to set, but he's just fine. She won't leave town until she has him. I could always tinker with their car if you think it's worth it, but now that Mike is dead—"

"Mike wouldn't have made a difference. He wasn't a very good mechanic anyway. And it's not like they'll need the car repaired. Once we get rid of the man, the woman will never leave." The lady sighs, and her chair squeaks. "Just do whatever you think is necessary. If they come down, I'll occupy them, but make it quick."

Rayna and I turn for the bedroom again, but my feet tangle together, and down I go. With a silent scream, I sprawl across the upper landing in plain view of Samuel and the woman. I mentally plead with Rayna, urging her to run, but of course she doesn't. She grips my ankles and tries to pull me back into the shadows, but it's too late.

"Grab them!" the woman squeals.

Footsteps pound up the stairs, and Samuel looms over us like some giant harbinger of doom. His meaty fists reach down, taking my arm in one hand and Rayna's in the other. With the ease of a child picking up sticks, he lifts us into the air and begins dragging us down the stairs. My blood runs cold when I see which door he's snatching us toward.

Looks like Rayna will get that morgue tour after all.

# Chapter Nine

### Rayna

All visions of escape evaporate after only a few minutes in the basement. Samuel left us down here without a word. He locked the door behind him, and that door is the only exit. Despite being a morgue, all the tools of the trade are absent, save for the single autopsy table. Not a bone saw or rib spreader in sight. Which means we are well and truly stuck.

"At least it's a nice temperature down here," Dalton grumbles as he slides down the wall and takes a seat.

He's ready to give up, but I don't know the meaning of the words. I give the door a final tug, then kick it with a scream before heading toward a metal cabinet that stretches from the floor to the ceiling. I'm sad to find the doors unlocked, because that means the contents aren't worth protecting. My sadness only grows when I discover this is where they store their canned goods.

I grab a can of peas and test its heft in my hand. "If we

shove a few of these into our socks, we could make a weapon."

"It's pointless."

"Hell, the cans are made of metal. Maybe we can fashion a blade." I throw the can to the floor, hoping it will burst open, but it only creates a dent.

"Didn't you hear me, bones? Don't waste your energy. We need to think of an actual plan."

"What do you think I'm trying to do?" With a scream, I grab another can and toss it at the wall. "I'm trying to find a way out of this fucking mess I got us into. I'm trying to fix it."

The tears threaten to come, but I refuse to cry. I grit my teeth and think about killing Samuel and his bitch of a mother, and the tears recede.

"Bones . . . come here." Dalton waves me toward him, and I can't help myself. I don't rush into his arms like some terrified maiden, but I reluctantly plop into his hold, where I melt.

"I'm only going to say this once, so make sure you're listening." I take a deep breath. "I'm sorry."

He brushes the hair from my face, then moves me in his lap until I'm straddling him and resting my forehead against his. "You really got us into it this time, huh?"

I nod.

"You know I'll get us out of it, though. Right?"

I nod again, because he will. He always does. This man has proven time and time again that I can count on him, even when the problem is of my own making. He'll fix this.

"Do you think I'll ever see Van Gogh again?" I whisper as I relax into him.

His hand traces lazy circles on my back. "I promise you

will. If I have to tunnel through the hellfire beneath this town to get to him, I'll do it."

"So no more talk of leaving him?"

Dalton shakes his head. "No, we aren't leaving this town until we've grabbed our son and wiped every one of these assholes from the earth."

A speaker crackles overhead, followed by an unfamiliar male voice. "You wish to do my family harm? That's not very nice."

"Neither is kidnapping people for your creepy town, jackass!" Dalton shouts at the ceiling.

The speaker crackles again, followed by laughter. "You think we're kidnapping you for our town? How cute. We only have plans for the woman, however. Your purpose . . . Well, it's almost All Hallows Eve, and I wouldn't want to spoil the surprise."

The speaker cuts off, silencing the man's laughter.

Dalton sighs and pulls me closer. "They're listening in. We can't even plot anything."

If they're listening . . . they might also be watching.

I press my lips against Dalton's ear and whisper, "Play along." The words are little more than a prayer lingering on an outbreath, so I hope he heard me.

A hum of excitement runs through me as I climb off Dalton's lap and go for the first metal door built into the wall. It comes open, and I slide the table from within. I pull back the sheet to reveal a fully nude man in his forties or early fifties. Bruising on his torso and abdomen suggests a pretty painful death, but I don't dwell on that. As much as I would love to examine this corpse and pull it apart, there is more important work to be done.

With a grunt, I grab the man's icy feet and tug him backward. He slides a few inches, but little more. I grunt and pull again, but I get less movement this time. "Little help?" I shout toward Dalton.

He scrambles to his feet and helps me pull the man to the floor. The corpse lands on the hard tiles with a sickening *splat*, and Dalton recoils. I hurry to the next door.

"Please don't disrespect our dead this way," the man says through the speaker. "This won't get you anywhere. Well, nowhere good."

Ignoring his crackling words, I snatch open the second metal door and pull out the table. Below this blanket, I find a young woman. She doesn't look much older than me. A Y-shaped incision mars her torso, cutting right between her small breasts.

Is this my fate?

"Bones, what are we doing?" Dalton asks. He stands at the woman's feet as I stare down at her, frozen. It's the first time I've ever considered my own mortality. Like . . . really considered it. And it's fucking me up.

I can't answer him, so I just step to the foot of the table and pull. With his help, we get her onto the floor and move her beside the man.

"You can continue these shenanigans if you wish, but bear in mind that you'll be cleaning up the mess you make." The speaker cuts off again, but now I know they can see us. Now I know that my plan will work.

The next bay is empty, but the bottom three tables all hold a surprise: three more bodies. These also bear an autopsy marking, like the woman, but they are considerably less fresh than the first two. The skin has shifted from a yellowish color to something more akin to gray. The flesh slips a bit as we pull them down to join their dead friends on the frigid floor.

"For a town that prides itself on preservation, they sure

did a shit job with these three," I say, loud enough for our listeners to hear. Working in silence, we situate the bodies into a line.

Perfect.

With a smirk toward the ceiling—I don't know where the cameras are, so I'm just guessing here—I turn to Dalton and raise my arms. "Now strip me. Let's have that orgy."

I expect the indignation from above to be instant, but Dalton is able to get the shirt past my bare breasts before the screeching begins.

"Her nakedness is an abomination! Her body is meant for my son, and no one else should see her! This is unclean! Filthy!" The woman's voice blasts through the speakers, and I fear the devices will shatter. But at least I'm getting a clearer picture now.

"So this is a family affair?" I say as my shirt drops to the floor. "It's going to be a bit uncomfortable to watch this with your kids, lady. Viewer discretion is strongly advised."

With a laugh, I go to my knees and begin unfastening Dalton's pants. He's never been a fan of having an audience, so I'm not surprised that he looks terrified. His dick, however, is more than ready. It springs from his boxers the moment I've lowered them.

As I take his warm, firm cock into my mouth, I reach behind me and grip the first dead man's dick. It feels like one of those slime tubes you get for three thousand tickets at an arcade. I enjoy the way it squishes in my clenching fist, a sharp contrast to Dalton's stiff cock ramming past my lips.

"Mike is a married man! Leave his penis alone!" the woman squeals through the speaker. When she speaks again, her voice is muffled. "Get down there, Francis. Stop them! You mustn't let that man soil our son's clean dove!"

Dalton grips my hair and hastens my tempo on his cock.

"Oh, are you worried I'll get her dirty? You're a little late, dear. She's already fucking *filthy*."

"And I'm no dove, bitch." I moan, then deep throat Dalton until I'm gagging on his girth.

He lets out a low groan that sends a shock of pleasure straight between my legs. I release the corpse cock and begin removing my shorts.

"I want you. I want you now," I say as I drop back on the bed made of bodies. Cold flesh rushes toward my skin, dampening my warmth and making me hotter all at once. "Fuck me, Dalton."

"No!" the woman screams, but it's too late.

Dalton has already dropped to his knees and rammed his face between my legs. I love it when he eats me out, but he knows we don't have time to focus on pleasure. He's just ensuring he doesn't ram into me dry. Because he under-stands the plan, and he's playing along, just as I asked.

Within minutes, we'll either escape from this hell . . . or die trying.

# Chapter Ten

### Dalton

Keeping my erection is a monumental task as I stare down at Rayna. She isn't the problem, though. She's perfection, with her dark hair and the fire in her eyes and the way her breasts swell with each breath she takes. The taste of her salty-sweet pussy still clings to my lips, which is definitely helping.

The dead bodies? Not so much.

I line myself up outside her entrance as I pretend a dead man isn't glaring right into my soul. His grey-green eyes stare sightlessly, but I feel like he's scrutinizing my every move.

Leaning forward, I turn his head toward the wall, and the woman's screeching rains down from the ceiling. She yells something about my unclean hands, but I can't hear her through the melee occurring around her. It sounds as if a brawl has broken out above us.

"Good," Rayna moans. "Let them tear each other apart while you tear *me* apart."

Oh, fuck. When she talks like that, she turns my dick into fucking rebar. I want nothing more than to pound into her until she's forced to beg me to stop, but there is still the issue of the dead people. It doesn't help that I feel cold fingers on my thigh as I scoot closer.

My eyes land on that warm place between Rayna's legs, and my will returns. If I have to rub against dead people to get me a little closer to heaven, so fucking be it. Besides, if we want them to rush down here so that we can fight, we have to give them a good reason.

And I think that's exactly what Rayna wants.

Gripping her thighs, I raise Rayna's ass and slide her entrance against the head of my aching cock. She arches her back, begging for me to enter her as her breasts jiggle from the movement. With a sharp yank, I impale her.

"Fuck!" she cries. Her fingers fly to her nipples, and she gives them a rough squeeze.

I lower my hand to her clit, but she pushes me away with a shake of her head.

"Use Mike," she says with a devious glint in her eyes. "Make me come with Mike's hand, Dalton."

"Oh, bones, you sick little fuck."

The smile on my face is completely contrived. If we weren't in this situation, I would argue with her. Yeah, she'd get her way in the end, regardless, but I have to put up a stink. Because this is just so far out of my comfort zone. But needs must, so I reach into the pile of bodies and pull up a hand.

On the third try, I find fingers that aren't as badly decomposed as some of the others. This is a feat, seeing how I'm currently fucking the shit out of Rayna as I search with only my hands. I really don't want to see Mike's face as I use his icy fingers to pleasure my girlfriend.

With each thrust into Rayna, I yank on the arm until it drapes over her stomach. I'm fairly certain I dislocated Mike's shoulder in the process, but I'll apologize later. I press the fingers against her clit, and her back arches off the body pile.

"The temperature difference . . . fuck, it's amazing," she moans. "You're going to make me come so hard!"

She screams this last bit, and that silences the speaker overhead. Bumps and bangs still reach us, but they've pulled the woman away from the mic, at least. Now it's a race.

Because I know my bones.

"You better fill me before they get down here," she whispers with a devilish smirk.

I nod. "Way ahead of you."

With a smile, she stretches her arms above her head, allowing her skin to caress the mass of carcasses beneath her. My disgust shifts to something more feral as I watch her move. I like the blood and violence. She likes the death. But there is something about the way she looks when she's reached the apex of pleasure, when she's surrounded by bodies and decay, that transcends what murder can do for me. Rayna is and always will be my greatest turn-on.

I pick up the speed with Mike's hand as footsteps barrel across the floor overhead. Her pussy clenches, squeezing me to the rhythmic beat of her heart. My balls draw up as her eyes close and she cries out, and we reach our edges simultaneously.

"I'm coming! I'm coming!" she screams as her thighs quiver against mine. In a state of blind ecstasy, she reaches back and grabs dead hands, dragging them over her body as she moans through the intense orgasm.

With a groan, I lean forward and fill her.

The upstairs door practically screams as someone wrenches it open. More footsteps pound down the basement stairs, and there's a scuffle just outside the door.

"Hurry, grab the cans!" Rayna whisper-shouts as she scrambles out from beneath me. She stumbles a bit on her way to the metal cabinet, then giggles. "Shit, I didn't consider how that post-orgasm haze might affect us."

Fuck. Neither did I. I feel ready for a nap, not a fucking fight.

But as the door swings open and Samuel's hulking frame steps into the harsh light, I force myself to my feet. With my dick swinging free between my legs, I lunge toward Rayna and catch two large cans as they fly toward my chest. I wheel on my heel and raise one of the cans, ready to strike, but Samuel doesn't charge us.

With his hands held out before him, he licks his lips and looks at the ceiling as he speaks. "Please cover her nakedness so that I can secure the two of you. My mother is very—"

"Shit, we don't even need the cans," I say with a laugh. "We have a cult full of nudity-phobics on our hands, bones."

Rayna giggles and sets her cans at her feet. "Aw, do my nipples frighten you, Sam?"

He clears his throat, still keeping his gaze fixed on the ceiling tiles. Why couldn't he have shown this much restraint before? If he'd avoided looking at Rayna from the beginning, we might have had a much different outcome. Granted, I still would have wanted to kill him, but still.

"Please," Samuel pleads. "Only my brother can see her when she's nude. Cover her up so that she's clean."

Rayna steps forward. "So you can't look and you can't touch, and you expect us to just obey you?"

Samuel takes a step back. "I've disabled your car, so

there's no escape. If he claims to love you, then he'll see the sense in this. He'll let you live, even if it means he has to die."

"You've been reading too many romance novels, dude." Rayna looks back at me and motions for me to follow her. "We're leaving, and there's nothing you can do to stop us."

"You can't leave. You don't understand."

"Dalton, let's go."

She steps back and grabs my hand, giving it a tug as she steps forward, but I don't budge. He has a point. If I loved Rayna, I would want her to live. And I do love Rayna.

But what he doesn't count on is my selfish nature. I love Rayna, but I refuse to allow another man to touch her. If that means we die together, so be it. And I know she wouldn't want it any other way.

I grip her hand and pull her into me, kissing her hard on the mouth. I break the kiss and look into her eyes. "We escape together or not at all, right?"

She smiles up at me and nods. "And that means Van Gogh too?"

"It means Van Gogh too. Now let's get out of here and find our son."

Hand in hand, we push past Samuel and head up the stairs. At the top, the woman sees us, lets out a scream, and faints on a dusty red couch. A man—I assume her husband —averts his eyes and hovers over the woman, fanning her face and muttering something about God.

"Give me your keys," I demand.

The gray hairs on his head quiver with rage as he stares down at the wheezing woman. "It won't do you any good. We've retrofitted all the vehicles with a kill switch. They can't leave the town."

Rayna laughs. "Who said we need it to leave town,

grandpa? We'll tear all through your city for as long as we want, and we'll do it naked. You won't even be able to watch us burn your house to the ground." Rayna steps closer, and he cowers. "Or maybe we won't burn it to the ground. Maybe we'll just drag our uncovered assholes on every kitchen counter. Then we'll fuck in your bed."

"Make it stop! Make it stop!" the woman wails.

"What do you want from us?" the man asks.

I scoff and step forward. "Oh, so *now* you want to be helpful? *Now?* Fuck you. Now we're going to make you assholes miserable on principle."

"Don't forget that I have your precious squirrel." Samuel's voice registers behind us, and we turn around. He's facing the opposite direction, but he still wants to be part of the conversation, I guess. "If you'll agree to leave town, I'll give him to you and fix your car."

Rayna and I look at each other. I'm a little disappointed, not gonna lie. Making these people miserable was starting to sound like a fun way to spend this Halloween.

"That's all we really wanted," she whispers.

The man clears his throat, but Samuel is the one who speaks. "Not her. She has to stay. She has to save my brother."

"I don't know what sort of creepy shit your brother is into, but this creepy shit is mine. No deal," I say. With that, I grab Rayna's hand and head for the front door.

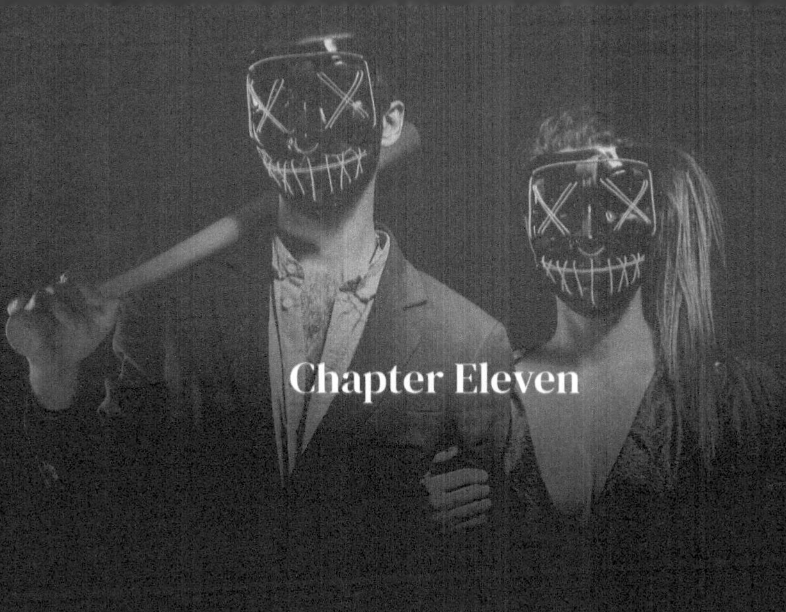

# Chapter Eleven

### Rayna

The pickup truck was easy enough to hot-wire, and we didn't even have to contend with the psycho family. We remained naked, and they remained inside. I'll mourn the loss of my clothing later. Right now, I'm just trying not to think about how many butts sat where my pussy now touches.

Dalton heads toward Samuel's house up the mountain. We hope our things are still there, including Van Gogh. And Raul. And the poor little rat-thong bikini that hasn't even gotten a name yet.

The carousel slides by on our left. The elderly woman and Mr. Fox are no longer seated by the gates. At least we know why the town feels so empty. It's because it is. These weirdos have somehow killed off the entire population of Oak Hollow, and no one is the wiser. A family of nutters, and that's saying a lot, coming from my mouth. I don't tend to judge.

I tap Dalton's shoulder as I stare out the window. "Let's

make a pit stop. I want to ride that wild-looking horse Grandma Moses shooed me away from."

"I don't know, bones." He shakes his head as he turns the truck around. "She said the horse was a bit too much for a little lady like you. What if it throws you? We're miles from any hospital."

"Oh, get fucked."

He grabs my hand and kisses it. "I can try to get hard again, but no guarantees."

He slides the truck into a parking spot, and we get out. It feels strange to walk through town in the nude, but it's the only way we can move around. Dalton even shed his shirt so that I wouldn't feel like the only member of our odd little nudist colony.

As if we belong here, we stroll up to the carousel and walk right up to the famed animal. In the bright afternoon sun, I can almost believe the old woman's tall tale. The dark horse looks very much alive, almost as if he might take off at any moment.

"Hop on and I'll man the controls," Dalton says.

With a nod, I allow him to help me mount the beast's back, which is higher than I can jump. He doesn't miss a chance to drag his finger through my bare pussy with a smirk. Once I'm seated, he brings the finger to his lips and sucks.

"Fuck, you always taste best when you're filled," he says with a groan.

I blow him a kiss. "You're so fucking filthy. Don't ever change."

His laughter disappears into the center of the carousel, and seconds later, the organ music grinds to life. Much like before, the deceivingly slow start gives way to pure chaos. Dalton has just enough time to leap onto the rotating platform before we reach a dangerous speed. He wobbles into a few horses in front of me before settling on a black pony.

"Your feet are dragging the platform," I say with a giggle.

He looks back at me, his hair flying around his face as we pick up speed. "I didn't think about how we'd get off this thing. More than our feet might be dragging around soon enough."

He has a good point, but right now, I don't care. I've never felt so free! Until I escaped a morgue and rode a taxidermy carousel in the nude, I couldn't grasp it. Now I never want to let go.

But as I tighten my grip on the post running through the horse, I'm holding on for a different reason. Unlike the horse on the last ride . . . this horse is starting to move. Something creaks and groans above me, and I look up at the rusted clump of metal attaching the horse to the machinery overhead. The other horses have been detached from the mechanism that moves them up and down, but my horse?

The metal screams, and the horse jerks upward. I'm flung down, but I grip the animal's neck for dear life. My ass remains seated, but only just. Dalton hears the commotion and turns around as the metal hook catches and pushes the horse down. I bounce when the rod reaches its lowest point and wants to keep going.

"It's going to buck me off!" I scream. "That bitch wasn't lying!"

Dalton fights against the centripetal force to make his way to me. With each step he takes, the horse seems to make another wild leap upward and downward. Metal groans overhead, and the platform whines beneath us.

"How did we not hear all this racket the first time?" I scream.

"There were a lot of fucking switches, okay? I might have pressed something I wasn't supposed to!"

His arm bands around my waist, and I take a deep breath. Then the horse begins to rise.

"It can't handle our combined weight!" I try to hold on to the horse, but Dalton tugs me down.

We crash against the horse to the right of the large bay, and its ass end gives way and rotates with us. When we land, our heads hang off the platform, mere inches from a bed of gravel as we move at light speed.

"Shit, I'm gonna hurl," Dalton groans, and I concur. If we don't get off this thing, we'll be the first humans in existence to commit suicide via a fairground kiddie ride. All the blood is rushing toward my feet.

The large horse continues its jerky up-and-down dance as I stare up and contemplate what it will feel like to be crushed by a ton of metal and tanned horse flesh. I can only think of one way this death could be improved, and that would be if Van Gogh were by our sides.

"I love you!" I shout to Dalton.

He squeezes my hand, lets out a guttural shout, and heaves our bodies from the platform. Gravel, sand, and God only knows what else scrape against my legs and back as I slide across the ground and come to a stop entirely too close to the wheel of death. With my bare breasts jiggling, I scramble to my feet and look around for Dalton.

A few feet away, he sits up with a groan and fingers a small gash on the side of his face. Blood coats his fingertips. Just as I reach his side, the merry-go-round gives a sickening groan, and the large bay crashes to the platform and slides inward. The thick metal rod breaks through the colorful bulbs lighting up the center mast, then lodges within the inner workings. After a few more clanks and groans, smoke begins to pour from the top.

"Shit, it's gonna catch fire," he says as he clambers to his feet. He grips my hand and pulls me away from the impending disaster.

Somewhere in the distance, a loud wail pierces the air, followed by a woman's voice. "The stables are burning! Save the horses!"

Dalton looks toward the voice and shakes his head. "Come on, bones. It's time to make our exit. Let's get Van Gogh and get the fuck out of here."

He tries to pull me with him, but I snatch my hand back as I spot a small figure running toward us.

"No, because *fuck* them. They tried to kidnap us, and they *did* kidnap our son. They want to kill you, and I have no desire to find out their plans for me." I fold my arms over my chest and refuse to take another step. "I'm staying right here. When they try to put out this fire, they'll have to do it with their fucking eyes closed."

Dalton sighs and returns to my side. "That old woman doesn't seem too bothered by our nakedness. Look at her. She's not slowing down."

Something explodes behind me, and I flinch, but I keep my gaze trained on the old woman hobbling toward us at . . . well, it's not the speed of sound, but she's doing her fucking best. She raises the taxidermy fox and wiggles him at us, and as she shouts something unintelligible, spittle flies from her mouth.

"Wow, she is pissed."

I scoff. "Super pissed. And I don't blame her. That's probably over sixty grand in taxidermy alone, and it's about to be reduced to ash. I feel a bit guilty, not gonna lie."

Dalton nods. "Yeah, maybe it would be best if we kept

moving. They'll be tied up with this for a while, and it will give us a chance to snoop."

"And fuck." I reach over and give his flaccid dick a squeeze.

I think we can knock at least one more item off that list before we evacuate this shit hole.

# Chapter Twelve

### Dalton

The house was locked up tight when we arrived, so I broke a window and let us in. It's not as if we have to worry about the Oak Hollow PD. They were probably first to go once the Psycho Family Robinson got it in their heads that they needed to kill every townsperson.

While I'm curious to know more about these people and what their damage is, my top priority is finding Van Gogh and getting us the fuck out of here. I've been doing my best to keep Rayna's mind occupied so that she can't think too long about how weird this place is, but if she starts thinking about it too much, we'll never get out of here. Not until she answers every question her brain can come up with.

We're currently in Samuel's bedroom. We already grabbed our things from the basement. Rayna wanted to dress, so I told her I'd wear my gym shorts in the event that one of us needed to strip quickly and scare off the weirdos.

God. I still can't wrap my mind around calling someone *else* the weirdos.

"Have you checked the bookshelf?" I motion to a shelf littered with taxidermy manuals and anatomy tomes. "Samuel didn't exactly strike me as the studious type. Maybe these are just for show?" I take a step toward the shelf, but the frustrated grunt from Rayna stops me.

"He's not in here," she says with a resigned sigh. She closes the lid of a trunk she's been digging through, then flops onto her ass. "Where could he be if he's not in this house? Where else can we look? We could be here for weeks."

She looks so forlorn and small, and it's killing me. I move toward the bed and sit on the edge of Samuel's very firm mattress, where I pull Rayna from the floor and into my lap. She melts in my arms, her warm breath fanning against my neck as I hold her.

"We'll find him. If I have to tie him down and force him to look at a Playboy to get the truth out of him, I'll find your squirrel." I kiss the top of her head. "It won't take weeks, either. If we have to spend more than another day in this *Dawn of the Dead* remake, I'll lose my shit."

A door slams near the front of the house, and Rayna and I freeze. The only hiding space is a tall wardrobe tucked in the corner. There is no closet in sight, and the bed is practically touching the ground, so there's no way we could cram ourselves underneath. I push Rayna toward the wardrobe, shove her inside, and tuck myself beside her before closing the door.

Holding our breath, we peer through the slats as the bedroom door flies open. Samuel pounds into the room, eyes narrowed, steam practically billowing from his ears. His fists clench and unclench at his sides as he glances around the room—at the bed, at the trunk, at the wardrobe where we hide—before raring back and kicking the trunk at his feet. Wood splinters and litters the floor.

Rayna's head slowly turns toward me, revealing her wide eyes. *What the actual fuck?* she mouths.

I turn back to the slats. Samuel has gone to the book-shelf now. He's speaking to himself as he paces back and forth, running his big hands through his hair, but I can't make out a word of what he says.

"Are they in there?" a man's voice calls from the front of the house.

Samuel shakes his head. "No sign of them. I think they were here, though. Probably looking for that squirrel."

Thank fuck I parked the truck in the forest at the head of the driveway. Rayna gives my hand a squeeze, likely thanking me for exactly that.

"Maybe they left town. You'll need to get back out there and—"

"They haven't left town," Samuel says, just loud enough to silence the man. He steps toward the bookshelf and pulls out a thick copy of some ancient medical book, which he opens. Inside the book is a hollow depression, and inside the depression—

"Van Gogh," Rayna whispers.

I wrap my arm around her shoulder and pull her against me. I'm not trying to quiet her, though. She needs me right now, and I'm letting her know I'm with her in the only way I can. Her shoulders tremble in my grasp, and as she tilts her head to the side, unable to witness the way Samuel handles her baby, a single tear falls onto my hand.

Rage coils under my skin. It winds into a tight ball,

waiting for the moment when I release the tension and allow it to spring forth, unchained. Unrestrained. And I will release it. By making Rayna cry, they all but guaranteed it.

"They die today, bones," I whisper in her ear. "All of them. Every one of them. They die today. For you."

Her trembling stops, and even though another tear falls down her cheek, a smile breaks through.

"I'm going back to the main house to check on your mother and brother," the man calls from the front of the house. "Will you be joining us for dinner, or would you prefer to remain here?"

"I'm coming with you, Pa!" Samuel shouts back as he wiggles Van Gogh. Then he tucks the squirrel into his back pocket and exits the room.

Rayna and I remain in the wardrobe until the crunch of tires on gravel fades to silence. We unfurl from the shadows and stand in the room, looking at the floor but seeing nothing.

I reach for her hand. "Come on, bones. Let's follow them and use the element of surprise."

She shakes her head and steps toward the bed. Her backpack slides off her shoulders and lands on the mattress. "No. The father said something about dinner, so I think we should wait until they're seated at the table. At least make sure Van Gogh isn't present before we attack."

I see what she's saying. If we spring a trap on them while they have Van Gogh in their possession, they will have the upper hand. We need to get him first.

"What should we do while we wait?" I ask. "We already fucked up their carousel."

Rayna's eyebrow rises as she sits on the bed and begins rifling through her bag. A mischievous smirk slides onto her face. "Step out of the room, and don't come back in until I tell you to."

An anticipatory sweat slicks my brow as I rise and exit the room. Rayna's surprises are usually well beyond the scope of what people consider normal. Even people like me. The shock is a small price to pay for the fantasy she fulfills for us both.

A few minutes pass before she calls for me to enter. When I open the door, my jaw nearly hits the floor. She's wearing the dreadful rat-thong bikini we purchased at the oddity shop.

"I am so fucking attracted to you, bones. You know that. But . . ." I search for the right words, but only one seems to do. "No."

"No? What do you mean?" She turns and wiggles her hips, showcasing the scaly rat tail dangling between her full ass cheeks.

When she faces me again, I finally realize how the bottoms tie together. The rat was skinned in a T pose, making it look like a rodent reenactment of the crucifixion across her pelvis. White ribbons attach to the hands and feet, then connect at her hips. The top isn't much better. A rodent head glares at me from the apex of each furry triangle struggling to cover her full breasts.

And yet, despite the grotesque ensemble, despite the fact that I've already drained my balls within the last six hours, my cock begins to strain against the front of my gym shorts.

Rayna has twice the screws loose that I ever had. In fact, since meeting her, she's unscrewed a few extras from me. I don't particularly like rodents of any kind, but I *do* like Rayna. Even as she sits on the edge of that small bed and pouts, the front of the taxidermy rat gives an obscured view of what I want, what I *always* want, even when it's behind something so macabre.

So I do what any insane boyfriend does for his even more insane girlfriend. My "no" becomes a "yes," and I hurry to her and push her onto her back. My lips trail down her neck and over her perfect breasts. Fur tickles my nose, but I ignore it and pretend it's anything other than what it is. I inch down her body until I'm between her legs, and the undergarment is even more horrifying up close. It's not even good taxidermy. It's a horror scene between her silky thighs.

"Couldn't we take these off and—"

"No, Dalton! Just eat me out!"

The woman has spoken.

My finger strokes the brown brindled coat as I grip the crotch of her underwear and pull it aside. The rat head flops to the side, its eyes meeting mine as I bring my chin to her slit. Eating out Rayna to the glowering and judgmental stare of a dead rodent wasn't on our adventure list, but I drop my gaze to what I really want and get to eating.

My tongue swipes her clit and electrifies her upper body. Her back rises off the bed, and her hands disappear in my hair as I devour her until she's screaming my name into the abyss. Her hips move against me, grinding and circling as she chases her pleasure. The corner of the bed knocks against the wardrobe, and it kicks open. Clothes tumble from inside. I'll have to clean that up later, once Rayna has finished soaking my face.

"I'm going to come, Dalton," she pants as her spine curves and her abdomen draws tight. Her thighs shake against the sides of my head.

"Come, bones," I growl against her slit.

And she does. She absolutely shatters the earth around us as she crests the most delicious peak I've created for her.

All I know is she soaks my chin with her pleasure, and I love how she tastes. I climb up her body from between her legs and kiss her, letting her taste how sinfully delicious she is.

"You feeling a little better now?" I ask with a smirk.

She sighs against my lips and smiles up at me. "Yes. Now let's go fuck some shit up and take back our son."

# Chapter Thirteen

**Rayna**

The sun sinks behind the trees as we exit the truck. Dalton did an excellent job of hiding it again, but I have a feeling they know where we are at all times. This nagging feeling of being watched follows me at every turn, and I wouldn't put it past them to have the entire town under surveillance.

"Do you think we should strip again?" I whisper. "If they're watching us move around town, that might help us conceal ourselves."

Dalton shakes his head. "Let them think we've let our guard down. Let them get cocky. If we need to whip out some dick and tits, we'll do it, but let's let them think they're safe for now."

I nod and keep walking beside him.

When we reach the end of the street, the carousel comes into view. I'm secretly happy to see that the horses were spared the worst of the flames, but I don't think they'll have it up and running anytime soon. Black char marks darken what remains of the canopy, and the entire center has been reduced to broken glass, melted plastic, and ruined machinery.

"I suppose the old woman is having dinner with them," I say with a shudder. "Three generations of complete nonsense for brains."

"Yet another reason I'm so glad we're both on the same page about no kids in our future. I have a feeling mixing our genetics could result in a similar outcome."

"I like taxidermy and dead shit. You like blood and murder. These are normal things to enjoy, Dalton. But we haven't wiped an entire town from the map or kidnapped . . . Well, I guess we technically kidnapped—"

"Exactly," he says, and I drop the topic, because fucking yikes.

Dalton turns us down another side street, and I'm glad he's handling the directions. I'm navigationally impaired— the very definition of passenger princess, if you will. If I'd been tasked with getting us back to their main house, we'd have taken a wrong turn at Albuquerque for sure. But like a scent hound on a trail, he leads us exactly where we need to go.

A few turns later, the large house looms in the distance, its bone wind chime clinking in the light breeze. At our walking pace, I have more time to notice other details, like the smiling carved pumpkins set along the railing. Flames flicker behind their open eyes.

"Should we knock on the door and say, 'Trick or treat!'? Or is that too much?" I whisper.

Dalton stops and pulls me into some bushes along a fence next door to our target. "Before we do this, I want you to promise me something. If they catch me, you have to let me go. You have to get out of here. Understood?"

I roll my eyes and cross my arms over my chest, but he keeps staring at me, waiting for a response. "Oh, you're serious? Well, fuck that. If you get caught, I'll set you free."

"Bones—"

"I didn't mince words, dude. I'm not leaving you here."

"Rayna."

The way he says my name, so clipped and final, tells me there's no room for argument here. Even if there were, this is the one time when my femininity can't get me what I want.

Footsteps stomp across wooden boards nearby, and Dalton and I freeze. Holding my breath, I peer through the shrubbery as Samuel clomps across the porch. He steps to the railing and grips it with his massive hands, leaning over the side and peering out at the darkening sky. I scan his figure for any sign of Van Gogh—a furry tail, the glint of a glassy eyeball—but I see nothing.

"He must have hidden him in the house," Dalton whispers.

Before I can whisper a response, the door clicks open, and the father steps into the porch light's glow. "Your brother continues to sleep. I fear we're running out of time."

I glance at Dalton and see that he's just as concerned as I am. His brother still sleeps? What the fuck does that mean? Is he in a coma or something?

"What if she isn't the one?" Samuel asks.

"Then we kill her and try again." The father shrugs and checks his watch, as if killing me is as mundane as reading the morning paper. "Dinner is almost ready. Go wash up."

The men retreat inside, leaving us alone in the bushes

once more. Shadows move behind the curtains, and we watch as they travel from room to room. Once the movement stops, we finally ease ourselves from our hiding place.

Stars twinkle in a cloudless sky as we creep across the dewy grass. As we draw nearer to the house, the distant clink of silverware on ceramic reaches our ears, coupled with the murmur of voices. The voices grow louder and clearer as we reach a bright window at the rear of the house. The window is too high for either of us to peer into.

Dalton squats and makes a basket with his hands, motioning for me to use him as a step. I place my foot on his woven fingers, then grip the windowsill as I rise.

The family sits at a large table, with the father and mother seated at opposite ends. The mother wears an angry scowl as she eats. The grandmother's back faces me, and across from her sits Samuel. His thick forearms rest against the table as he chews.

My eyes scan their surroundings. Dishes filled with green beans, roasted chicken, and various other items line the side table against the wall. A large grandfather clock ticks close to the doorway leading into the dining room. A few taxidermy rabbits sit beside a vase of fake flowers on a shelf.

But I see no sign of Van Gogh.

I motion for Dalton to lower me, and he does. "He isn't in there," I whisper.

"We'll have to search the house. Would we be able to sneak in now?"

I glance up at the window again. "The open doorway presents a bit of a problem, but as long as we don't go near the dining room, we could search some of the other areas while they eat. I don't know how much time we'll have, though."

Dalton nods. "Maybe we should just find a place to hide until they go to sleep. Then we can search. Quietly."

It's not the greatest plan, but it's better than anything I can come up with on short notice, so I grip his hand to let him know I'm in agreement. He hoists me up once more to ensure everyone is still seated. Once I have that confirmation, he lowers me, and we tiptoe through the side yard.

Using hand signals, I ask if he thinks we should enter the house via the side door. Using hand signals, he motions back that he's going to throw a fastball. In reality, I have no idea what those signals mean, but I'm going into this house whether he likes it or not.

I hurry up the steps before he can reach out and grip my arm. The door eases open with a high-pitched whine. Every cell in my body freezes as I wait for the conversation to stop, for the forks to cease scraping the plates, but as the noises continue, I finally relax.

"They're oblivious," I whisper to Dalton, but he just stares up at me.

Rolling my eyes, I grip his hand and pull him into the house. Shadows wrap around us as we close the door and trap ourselves in the laundry room. A washer and dryer sit silent and still beneath a long white shelf holding laundry detergent and a box of dryer sheets. I never pegged them as a Downy family. They seem more like the Bounce types.

"Stop studying their cleaning supplies and start finding the squirrel," Dalton whispers in my ear. He gives my ass a light pat, urging me forward.

But my feet are glued to the floor. I'm unable to move as footsteps pound in our direction. We freeze and wait for the sounds to pass. Once things grow quiet once more, we creep toward the door and dare to peek beyond our hiding spot. Across the hall, water runs behind a closed door.

"Someone is in the bathroom," I whisper to Dalton. "Think we can sneak past?"

He nods, then slips past me and steps into the dark hall-way. Holding my breath, I step forward and follow him. I have no clue where we're going, but we're going together.

# Chapter Fourteen

### Dalton

A dust bunny wiggles beside my nose with every breath I take beneath this bed. Rayna snuggles against my side as we try to remain as still as possible. Ma and Pa Psycho snore a few feet above us, but we keep counting the seconds until morning. It's all we can do at this point.

The snooping started out great. We managed to hit every upstairs room without getting caught, and we planned to sneak back downstairs as they enjoyed dessert. We'd hide until they retired for bed, then explore the downstairs rooms while they slept. Unfortunately for us, they chose to skip dessert. When the elder parents ventured upstairs, we hardly had time to squeeze beneath their bed.

Rayna extends her legs, wincing as her toes point. After lying on these wooden slats for hours, she's likely stiff as a sock from my early twenties. It feels like it's been hours, at least. But then I realize she isn't just stretching. She's wiggling sideways and easing out from under the bed.

I grip her hand and squeeze until she looks at me. I shake my head, silently begging her to stay put, but she just rolls her eyes and starts scooting again. Not wanting her to take such a risk on her own, I do the only thing I can and follow her.

Once we're out from under the bed, Rayna steps toward the foot and grips the solid footboard. Moonlight filters through the curtains and plays over her features as she scowls down at the sleeping couple.

Then she lowers her shorts.

"Bones, what are you doing?" I whisper.

Gripping the footboard once more, she bends at the waist and peers at me over her shoulder, biting her lip in that seductive way that drives me wild. "Fuck me, Dalton. Fuck me, but don't wake them up. And when you're ready to come, I want you to do it in his hand." She points at the father, whose hand dangles off the side of the bed.

"I can probably get it up, but I doubt I can—"

Her eyelashes flutter. "Try?"

Okay. I think I can manage that.

I lower my shorts, then grip her hips and focus on the curve of her ass as she reaches between her legs and brings my hardening cock toward her entrance. We suck in a breath at the same time as we feel that first sweet moment when I push inside her. The combined sound causes Ma Psycho to stir, and the woman turns onto her side. Rayna and I freeze, waiting to see if she'll wake, but she doesn't.

My confidence grows, and fuck, Rayna feels amazing. I push forward and earn a small whimper from her. Leaning forward, I shush her, but my warm breath against her neck sends goosebumps springing from her soft skin. Unable to stop myself, I lower my mouth and nip her.

"Fuck," she whispers, and the woman on the bed shifts again.

"Quiet, bones. Don't wake them up if you want me to finish."

That's easier said than done when I push fully into her again. Her pelvis bumps the footboard, and the motion travels up the bed, pushing the headboard into the wall. Looking back, she grips her bottom lip between her teeth and pushes against me, begging me to hurt her.

I pick up the speed, pulling her hips away from the bed so that we don't make more noise than we need to. Her beautiful ass jiggles with each forward thrust, and as her head lolls, I see that her eyes are already rolling in her head. I move my hands to her shoulders and ram her harder. On a silent moan, she pushes her hand between her legs and batters her clit to the rapid tempo of my hips against her ass.

Seconds later, her knees begin to shake and her pussy clamps down on my dick. She breathes through it instead of crying out, but I can tell she can't hold out much longer. Normally I'd hold her here and keep fucking her until she screams, but that isn't wise, given our current situation.

"Come in his hand," she whispers, and I pull out of her, because what? But before I can stop her, she's gripped my cock and started leading me toward the sleeping man's open hand at the edge of the bed.

"Bones, what are you—"

It's no use. She starts jacking my dick, using her pleasure as lube. It feels incredible, and with each rapid stroke, she's dragging me closer to detonation. It's too late for thoughts of dead grandmothers as a jet of come blasts from my dick and splats across his skin. Once I've spurted the last of it, she releases me and steps closer to the bed.

I grip her arm to stop her. "I think that's enough."

Like a wisp of smoke, she twists out of my hold and leans closer to the man's sleeping face. She grips a lock of her hair in one hand and dangles it over his nose. My own nose begins to itch as she teases his skin with her silky locks, and my face begins to twitch. And so does his.

My stomach lurches as his hand floats toward his face. Rayna hops backward, missing the globby fingers by mere millimeters as they rise. In slow motion, we watch the sticky goo smear over his cheek, nose, and finally, his lips. He licks the latter a few times before turning onto his side and pulling his wife closer with the dirty hand.

Rayna covers her mouth to stifle her laughter. I cover my mouth to hold back the vomit.

When she's had her fill of laughing at this mess we've created, she grabs my hand and pulls me toward the door. We exit the room and pad on silent feet down the hallway. At the top of the stairs, I stop and pull her closer.

"We should split up," I say into her ear. The words have hardly left my mouth before she begins shaking her head. "Bones . . . we have a greater chance of finding him if we split up. If they come after you, just flash some nip."

Her eyes fill with tears because we both know this isn't risky for her. They need her for some sick reasons of their own making, but I'm expendable.

"I'll be just fine." I reassure her with a kiss pressed against her temple. "You search—"

"No. We aren't splitting up. You never split up in a horror flick. That's survival one-oh-one."

I let out a sigh, then nod. "We have to do this. For Van Gogh. Just promise me that if shit goes south, you'll head for the truck."

She sets her jaw.

"Promise me, bones, or we'll stand right here until these assholes wake up at the crack of dawn."

Her shoulders droop, and her raised chin finally lowers a few inches. "Fine. I promise I'll head for the truck if shit goes south."

"Good girl." I rub her shoulders and press my forehead to hers. "You search the left side of the downstairs, and as soon as you're finished, meet me by the back door. Whoever finds Van Gogh first should go straight there. If I don't show up by sunrise, you know what to do."

She nods, gives me a quick peck on the mouth, then disappears down the hallway, leaving me alone on the landing.

Why do I get the sneaking suspicion she's already found a loophole?

# Chapter Fifteen

**Rayna**

**D**alton has lost his mind if he thinks I'll abandon him. If I'm willing to go through all this trouble for a fucking taxidermy squirrel, he must realize the lengths I'll go to in order to keep him in my life. There is only one way Dalton can rid himself of me, and that's by securing himself passage behind the pearly gates. Fat chance of that happening. No, we'll both be firmly seated on the train to hell, side by side. I'll make sure of that.

The stairs creak as Dalton descends, and my spine ratchets straighter with each wooden groan. Sweat slicks my palms. And my forehead. Hell, sweat slicks everything on my body, if I'm being real. I'm a nervous wreck as I wrap my hand around the banister and start down the stairs.

Yet I've never felt more alive.

"Missed my calling as a burglar," I whisper as Dalton and I part ways.

I meander into a dark office. Strands of moonlight cut through the blinds and gouge bright gashes into a desk against the far wall. Ledgers pile high on its surface. A computer from the nineties sits amid the stacks of papers and bindings, its fat black face staring blankly up at me as it drowns forgotten. I run my finger through a thick blanket of dust on the tufted armchair in front of the desk. No one has been in this room for ages.

Stepping closer to the desk, I spy a manilla folder that looks a bit fresher than the rest. I pluck it up, unable to contain my curiosity, and flip to the first page. It's a medical record for someone named Jebediah Hollows.

As I read the doctors' and nurses' scrawled notes, a picture begins to form. One of a desperate family who was unable to accept a pretty horrible diagnosis. The medical staff repeatedly mentions the way the mother and father lose their grip on reality. Superstitions morphed into dangerous beliefs, and by the time Jebediah succumbed to his disease—some sort of autoimmune issue, though it's wholly unclear in the notes—the family was convinced he was merely hibernating until a cure could be provided.

I close the manilla folder and place it back on the desk. A lump has formed in my gut, and I can't help but feel a little compassion for the family. Not enough compassion to want to help them, but enough to feel bad for letting Dalton come in the father's hand.

Then again . . . those assholes took my squirrel. Fuck them.

I pull out the drawers and sift through their contents, but Van Gogh isn't within the dusty shadows. The cabinet standing against the wall receives brief consideration before I shake my head and leave the room. Only ghosts of a family reside in there.

As I step into the hallway once more, the distant sound of toppling cloth reaches my ears, followed by a suppressed grunt. My initial urge is to go to Dalton and see what sort of mess he's gotten into, but my forward momentum halts the moment I take the first step. Perched on the mantel above the fireplace, surrounded by family pictures and a few unlit tea lights, stands Van Gogh.

Hurrying to him on silent feet, I nearly trip over the rug sprawled across the floor. I steady myself on the couch and continue toward my most beloved possession. The moment my fingers graze his patchy fur, I pull him into me and breathe in his ancient, greasy perfume. I imagine this is what a mother must feel like when she holds her baby, breathing in that infant smell. A human child could never elicit this emotion from me, but this taxidermy squirrel holds the keys to my heart. Well, some of them. The rest are held firmly within the hands of—

"Dalton," I breathe as I look up and register him standing in an open doorway.

He doesn't look at me. In fact, his back faces me as he steps out of the room. His hands are raised as he backpedals, one slow step at a time, into the living area. I slip into an alcove beside the fireplace and hunker down in the shadows to bear witness to whatever is happening.

"Where's your woman?" a male voice says, and I recognize it as Samuel's voice before he steps fully into the moonlight blaring through the window. "We need her. She's the only chance my brother has."

I wince, because the only chance his brother had was a miracle, and that ship sailed about three years ago. The medical files ended with his death, which this family still hasn't accepted.

Dalton shakes his head and laughs. "Rayna is miles from here by now. I'm merely a decoy, sent to keep you assholes busy so that she could escape."

"Why wouldn't the two of you just escape together?"

"Well . . . I mean . . ."

I roll my eyes. Dalton is handsome, strong, and incredibly good in bed, but he's not the brains of our duo, that's for sure.

Samuel pushes forward, and that's when I spot the shotgun aimed at Dalton's chest. Perhaps I've judged him a bit harshly. I'm not so sure I'd be thinking clearly with a double barrel leveled on me, either.

"Just tell us where she is, and I'll make this easy on you. I promise," Samuel says, and the sincerity in his voice is almost believable. "You can be the last sacrifice. Give us the girl, and we'll take very good care of her."

*Why isn't Dalton ripping off his clothes?* I think to myself, but then I realize he never had the chance. Samuel must have gotten the drop on him in the room, preventing him from whipping out his dick.

I lick my lips and remember the promise I made to Dalton. If he were captured, I agreed I would go for the truck.

But I never promised I would leave him.

# Chapter Sixteen

## Dalton

Wherever Rayna is, I hope she's safe. That's the prevailing thought as I allow Samuel to tie my arms to a chair in the corner of a massive bedroom on the first floor. A bed stands by the window, the gauzy curtains draping over the canopy top catching bits of moonlight, but I can't make out the figure resting in the center of the mattress. They're a dark shadow, obscured by the curtains.

Once Samuel has tied down my wrists and ankles, he calls for his parents to enter the room. They join him in front of me, followed by the grandmother.

"Are murders always a family affair for you weirdos?" I ask.

The mother's brow furrows. "Murder? We don't commit murder. Sacrifice isn't the same thing."

"Murder is murder, asshole. Just admit that you get joy from killing people. It's not so bad." I smile up at her and try to wiggle my wrists free, but it's no use. I'm tied down too tightly.

"Don't let him confuse you, Samuel. We know why we do this. That's all that matters." Ma Psycho sidles up to her son and wraps an arm around his shoulder. "Once we have the girl, the ritual can begin. We'll have your brother back. Won't it be glorious?"

I blink up at them, but I don't interrupt this weird moment. Maybe I can learn something that will help me.

"Where's the squirrel?" the father asks.

Samuel motions to me. "We don't need it anymore. We have him."

"Now isn't the time to get cocky. Get the squirrel and bring it in here," the father says, and I'm surprised when Samuel trudges out of the room like a five-year-old who's just been informed they're grounded. The father turns back to me. "Where did she go? She's still in this house, isn't she?"

I shrug and smile up at him. "Couldn't tell you. I told her to run if I got hemmed up, so she's probably miles away from here by now."

"Without you or the squirrel?" He laughs down at me.

"Well, without him," Samuel says as he comes back into the room. "The squirrel's gone."

Now it's my turn to laugh. If Rayna found Van Gogh, she probably *is* miles away. Good for her.

The mother steps closer now, and I can see just how deep each wrinkle sinks around the sides of her mouth. In the low light, she looks like a bulldog. "What's so funny? The sacrifice occurs on Halloween night, whether we have the girl or not. Your death gives him another year tethered to our world."

"What, and you think Rayna's pussy will wake him up?

Lady, he's dead." I laugh a little louder, not because this is particularly funny, but because I don't want them to hear what I hear.

An engine. And it's drawing closer.

Seconds later, the room fills with light as headlights aim toward the window. I brace myself as the wall explodes in a burst of glass, wood, and sound. The truck's hood crumples as it crashes into the bedroom and knocks a dresser into a shower of splinters. Furniture flies across the room and collides with more furniture and possibly bodies. I can't see anything through the debris cloud. Incredibly, every bit of the flying shrapnel misses me.

Rayna bursts from the cab as the dust begins to settle, her squirrel clutched tightly in her right hand. "Did you miss me, bitches?"

I look around. The initial explosion knocked down all four of the psychos, who now groan on the ground as they try to register what just occurred. The grandmother clutches her fox and cries, and the mother looks like she might have struck her head. Blood oozes from a gash beside her eye. The father lies motionless. Samuel is the first to stand, but Rayna has both of my hands untied before he finds his feet.

"Hurry," I whisper. "We have to get out of here while they're still in shock."

Rayna keeps working on the binding on my left ankle while I work on the right. "Get out of here? I didn't come back just to save you, Dalton. These pieces of shit are going to die."

Samuel groans and leans against the wall. Chunks of plaster paint his skin in places, and several small cuts create red tracks through the white. When he sees that his father isn't moving, he drops to his knees beside him and begins rendering aid.

The moment my legs are free, I leap from the chair and grip the shotgun lying near the grandmother. She whimpers and scoots backward, clutching her fox to her chest. I don't have the heart to terrify her, so I whip the barrel toward the mother.

"On your feet," I say. "Looks like plans have changed."

She looks past me, at the bed currently resting at an odd angle. I pass the gun to Rayna because my curiosity has me in a chokehold. Then I make my way to the bed.

Two of the frame's legs broke off in the initial impact, casting the mattress at a downward angle at the foot. I step toward the head and peel back the curtain. Lying on the bed is a body in surprisingly good condition. The lips have begun to peel back, showing the teeth more than they should, but other than that, he does look like he might get up and walk. Thick blonde hair drapes his forehead. He wears a suit, and he can't be much older than Samuel is now.

I can see how a desperate mother could get confused. That doesn't explain how the insanity and desperation spread, however.

"Can't you see that he's still alive?" the mother pleads.

"Can't you see that you need some intensive grief thera-py?" Rayna quips. "Lady, he's dead. I get that you think my pussy is magic, but I can promise you that I do not have the Lazarus Labia. He ain't coming back from that."

I open my mouth to encourage her to tread lightly and have a little compassion. I mean, this is her son. But the woman speaks first.

"Please, if you'll just let us perform the ritual, you'll see." She goes to stand, but Rayna is having none of it. She swings the barrel toward her head, forcing her to stay seated or get walloped. She chooses to stay seated.

I step closer to Rayna and place my arm around her waist. "There's a new ritual in Oak Hollow, I'm afraid, and it's being held by the Halloween Harvesters. Nice to meet you."

Rayna giggles and passes the shotgun back to me. "This is going to be the best Halloween yet!"

# Chapter Seventeen

### Rayna

We secure everyone's hands and feet, then lead them toward the master bedroom upstairs, away from the body of their dead relative. Everyone is mostly coherent, save the father. I'm fairly certain he's bleeding internally. He slips in and out of consciousness at the back of their daisy chain.

The mother groans as she takes a step forward and is forced to drag her husband's limp body. "He's dying. If we don't get him some help, he won't survive."

"Funny that you think your survival is our goal," I mutter.

The father comes to again. He gets on his hands and knees and crawls behind his family. I aim the shotgun beside him and pull the trigger. Shrieks erupt, including a high-pitched screech from Dalton as he whips around.

"Sorry," I say with a shrug of my shoulders. "He isn't moving fast enough."

Dalton snatches the gun from my hands and motions for

the others to file into the room. They do as instructed, even going so far as to sit in the chairs we set up in front of the bed. If the mother knew what I had up my sleeve, she'd have run screaming from the house, shotgun aimed at her stupid head or not.

When they're all seated nicely, I begin tying them down as Dalton points the gun at the grandmother. That's enough to keep them in line, and she doesn't need to be tied down at all. She's done little more than hold the fox and whimper since I arrived.

The father's head lolls to the side, and a trickle of frothy foam oozes from the side of his mouth. It's pink, meaning he's got some serious internal injuries going on. His hands are cold as I tie them down, and he's definitely in the process of dying. We'd better hurry this up before we lose a quarter of our audience.

I hurry to the foot of the bed and begin removing my shirt. That earns an immediate squeal from the mother. She clamps her eyelids shut and turns her head away from us.

"I won't watch!" she shouts. "You can force me to sit here, but I won't witness your perversions. It's an affront to our beliefs!"

I scoff and lower the hem of my shirt. I'm so glad I made a pit stop at the morgue before plowing into the side of their house. It's also good that the mother reminded me to grab my things from the truck. After giving Dalton a kiss on his cheek and telling him I'll be right back, I hurry to the bedroom downstairs.

A soft *tick-tick-tick* drifts from the truck's otherwise silent engine as I enter the room. I clamber over the bed to reach the driver's side door, only pausing long enough to spare Jebediah a glance. It's all I have the courage for because he really looks like he could sit up and speak at any moment. If I hadn't viewed the medical records myself, I'd almost believe he was still in there too.

But he's not. That much is clear when I grab my bag from the truck and use my knife to make a small incision in his wrist. The dead flesh doesn't spread and fill with red the way live flesh would. I briefly consider dragging the corpse to the master bedroom and turning this into a threesome, but it doesn't feel right. Not many things feel wrong to me, so when they do, I listen.

After securing my bag on my shoulders, I stuff Van Gogh safely into his inner pocket and bid Jebediah farewell. Back in the bedroom, Dalton sits on the edge of the mattress as he picks dirt from his nails with the end of a silver letter opener. Our (literally) captive audience is seated and secured.

Now it's time to put on a show.

I set my bag beside Dalton on the bed and begin digging around inside. From the shadowy depths, I pull two silver devices that look like something from a torture film. Dalton doesn't know what they are, but the mother does. She begins wailing immediately because she knows what I intend to do.

"You can't make me watch! You can't!" she screams. "Even if my eyes are forced open, I'll turn my head!"

I slide off the bed with a laugh. "Lady, I'll ram a rod alongside your spine to ensure your cooperation if I have to. My boyfriend and I plan to entertain you assholes, and I'll be damned if any of you will opt out. Now, we can do this the easy way or the hard way." I jingle the metal contraptions, and she shuts her eyes.

"Have it your way," Dalton says with a shrug.

He hops down from the mattress and grips the woman's head between his hands. I imagine what it would be like if he squeezed until something cracked, and that's enough to get me excited. I step forward and ram the prongs beneath her upper eyelid. The prongs scrape along the slippery globe, and she lets out a guttural scream.

"If you'd hold still, it sure would hurt a lot less," Dalton says.

I slip the lower set of prongs beneath her eyeball, then begin ratcheting the dial on the side of the device, forcing her eyelids fully open.

A bubble of giddy laughter slips out of me. "Good grief, it looks like her eyeball could fall right the fuck out of her skull."

She screams again, earning more laughter from me as I set to work on her second eye. Moments later, she's been turned into a fucking stalk-eyed fly. Her peepers are popping like they've never popped before, I'm sure. Then she turns her head.

I sigh and step toward the foot of the bed as I remove my shirt. "I'll give you an option, lady. Either you can watch us fuck, or you can watch as I drag your son's corpse into the room and shove it into every hole I have, piece by chopped-off piece."

"You wouldn't defile him in such a way," she breathes.

"She absolutely would, and I would help." Dalton smiles at her. "Eyes on us, Ma Psycho."

With a grin, I pull the knife from my bag and hand it to Dalton. The father has a moment of clarity when he sees it, and he struggles against his ropes. But he has no need to worry. It's not meant for him.

I lie back on the bed as Dalton removes my shorts. I'm not wearing panties, so he drags his tongue through my slit one time before stepping away. As my thighs spread and showcase my pleasure, the mother begins to cry.

When I look up, I realize why. Her husband is currently half-dazed, but he's locked in on my pussy. The growing lump in the crotch of his pants tells me he's not so against this.

"You like looking?" I coo toward the man. I smack my hand against my cunt and drag my fingers through my wetness. "Yeah, you like it, don't you?"

"Why are you forcing us to watch this?" Samuel finally asks.

"You're exempt," Dalton says.

He drops the knife on the bed, rips off his shirt, and rushes to Samuel. He begins wrapping the shirt around Samuel's head, obscuring my body from his view. In the heat of the moment, I guess he forgot about his jealousy. It's kind of hot to see him so flustered, though.

Once Samuel can no longer glimpse my body, Dalton returns to the bed and takes up the knife again. "Turn over, bones. Let me bleed you."

The words rush straight between my legs and drive me wild. I flip onto my stomach, with my head facing our audience, and raise my ass in the air, hoping he'll add a new scar to the raised lines on my ass. It's my favorite because I get to feel the sting for weeks. Every time I sit down, I'll be reminded of this moment.

As if he read my mind, he presses the blade against my right ass cheek and drags downward, applying enough pressure to break the top layer of skin without driving too deep. The heat is instant and heavenly.

The father groans, and his head tips back as he loses consciousness again. The mother seems to calm a bit, almost taking an interest in our actions as Dalton runs his hand through the blood on my ass. When he brings the bloody mess between my legs, she's practically intrigued.

But it's not enough. Something about this just isn't *enough*.

I look back at Dalton with a pout. "Are you sure we shouldn't add a third? I mean, more blood is always better, don't you think? And it *is* Halloween, technically."

"I'm watching! Don't bother my Jebediah while he's resting," the mother pleads.

It's so funny that she thinks I'm talking about her son, but she must have missed the part about the blood. Of which he has none.

No, I'm thinking of bleeding someone else entirely. And with a sigh, Dalton agrees.

# Chapter Eighteen

### Dalton

We hoist the father onto the bed and tie his arms and legs to the bedposts, rendering him spread eagle. Ma Psycho is having a complete come apart, thrashing against her restraints and throwing her head around until one of the speculums tears away her left eyelid. The skin hangs in flaps by the rolling iris.

The father is much more compliant, though he's already firmly seated on his train to hell. He's more dead than alive at this point, but that's okay. We don't need him to partici-pate. We just need him to bleed.

Rayna straddles his waist, and I only allow this because he's still dressed and mostly incoherent. This is the closest I will ever let a living man come to what belongs to me. He gargles on pink foam as Rayna raises his sleep shirt and reveals dark bruising along his abdomen. Large purple marks brand his skin, and his gut has swollen enough to give him the appearance of a potbelly.

"I wonder what we'll find inside?" Rayna nibbles her

bottom lip in a devious grin. "A lacerated liver? Maybe a severed spleen or a ruptured rectum!"

Rayna slides off his lap once his belly is fully exposed. She takes a seat at his left side, and I perch on the edge of the mattress at his right, giving the mother a good view of her husband. The woman sucks in a breath as Rayna raises the blade above the man's midsection.

But then Rayna stops.

"Maybe we should give them a chance to repent," she says.

I blink at her. "What?"

"I dunno. It just feels wrong. This guy is as good as dead, and he and his wife deserve it, but there's still hope for the other two."

"Rayna, they wanted to sacrifice me and force you to fuck their dead son. Exactly which part of that screams redemption arc for you?"

She considers this, then shakes her head. "I'm cool with bleeding out the dad and torturing the mom, but the others deserve a chance to—"

"Yes!" the mother screams. "Yes, this could still work. Use my husband as the sacrifice. We can still revive my boy."

Samuel adjusts in his seat. It's the first time I've seen the man sweat since meeting him, so that means something about this current interaction is unnerving him. He grumbles something toward his mother, but I can't make it out.

"I do mean it, Samuel!" she screeches in response. "You were always jealous of Jebediah. Jealous! You weren't chosen, and he was meant to inherit everything. I should have sacrificed *you*. Why couldn't it have been you?"

The grandmother clutches the fox to her chest and rocks back and forth. A gentle whimper eases out of her as she begins to weep. Samuel's arm reflexively jerks in her direction in an effort to comfort her, but the bindings hold him in place. This show of compassion and care only infuriates the mother more.

"Stop coddling her," she snaps toward Samuel. "We're so close to your brother's resurrection. We can't stop now. Your father could be the key!"

I've heard about all I can stand to hear. I rise from the bed, wrench a satin pillowcase from its pillow, and stuff it into Ma Psycho's flapping mouth. "Do you ever shut the fuck up? Bitch, your son is dead. I can kill everyone in this room as Rayna grinds on his shriveled dick, and he will still be dead. The fact that you're willing to throw away your husband's life and shit on your remaining son is beyond comprehension. You're cooked, bitch. Now stop squealing and stick your fucking feet to the fire."

She's screaming something behind the makeshift gag, and I'm thankful I can't hear any of it. I step closer to Samuel as Rayna's observation finally hits me as well. He is a product of the sickness, but he isn't sick. He still has a chance, and so does his poor grandmother.

"Rayna, cover up," I say as I reach for Samuel's blindfold. Once she's pulled a throw over her chest, I pull the mask away from his eyes. I need to see that he understands what I'm about to say. "I want you to take the old woman and get out of here. Away from Oak Hollow. Can you do that?"

Samuel sets his jaw and nods as tears threaten to spill from his blue eyes.

"Do you understand what I'm telling you?"

He nods again. "I'm ready to leave this all behind. I can't do this anymore. I've wanted it to be over for so long, but I didn't know how."

"You know I can't let them live." I motion to his parents, and he nods again. "I can't even promise to make it quick."

"I can promise it won't be," Rayna mutters.

Samuel licks his lips and looks at the bed, though I'm thankful his gaze lands on his father and not Rayna. "Make it quick for him. We all did this for her. We loved Jebediah too, but we knew he wouldn't come back. She just couldn't accept it."

The mother screams something, but I talk over her muffled pleas. "I wish I could say I hope we don't cross paths again, but something tells me we might. It's a sickness, Samuel. Just make sure you choose better victims next time."

He tries to chuckle, but the gravity of the situation won't let it happen. His chest just jerks, caught on a half-sob. But it lets me know he understands that he can't come back here. He can't save his parents. And he wants to, even though he knows they don't deserve it.

I walk around to the back of the chair and untie his hands. Rayna seems more than pleased, and for the first time, I no longer feel threatened by Samuel. She had the opportunity to take her repaired squirrel and get the hell out of here, but she came back.

For me.

I had decided to wait until we were out of Oak Hollow to do this, but I see no better time. While Samuel goes to his grandmother's aid, I head straight for Rayna's side of the bed and kneel. I have no ring. I have no special speech prepared. I just have this undying love for a woman who is my everything and my all.

"Bones?" I look up at her, at the way the rising sun casts a pale orange glow across her skin, and it takes my breath away. "Rayna, I'm more in love with you now than I ever have been, but I'm nowhere close to loving you as much as I ever will. There is not a day that goes by when you aren't my first and last thought, plus most of my thoughts in between. I don't have a ring, but I'll get one. I just need to know . . . will you marry me?"

Ma Psycho bellows something and begins rocking her chair until it falls to its side. Samuel helps his grandmother to her feet and tries to assist her toward the door, but the old woman ducks out of his hold and runs toward the side of the bed.

Directly toward me.

The shock at how fast she moves is so great that I'm unable to get to my feet. Everything happens too quickly. She hurries forward as her right hand punches into the deep pockets dangling from her shoulder wrap. Her left arm grips her fox. I have no time to move as metal catches light. Before I know what's happening, a gleaming glint flashes in front of my eyes . . .

And then Rayna screams.

# Chapter Nineteen

## Rayna

The old lady pushes a ring into Dalton's face as I toss my shirt to the floor and throw myself into his arms. She nearly topples over as he hugs me to his chest, so I reach out to steady her—and get a better look at that ring.

"It was a gift from my late husband," she says. She holds the glistening clump of diamonds toward me. One round stone sits in the center, surrounded by a halo of smaller stones. The band is scuffed from age, and the metal's shine has worn away, but that almost makes it more special. More . . . me. It's something Dalton and I could never afford, not even if we decided to settle down and be normal.

It's something beautiful and perfect.

It's something I don't deserve.

My smile fades as I push the ring back toward the old woman. "It's beautiful, but I can't accept that. We're the reason your stables caught fire, and it wouldn't be right."

Never mind that we're also about to kill her son and daughter-in-law.

She grins and pushes back. "You're finally setting my grandson free. That more than makes up for it. As long as I have Mr. Fox?" She pats the animal's head and sighs. "I think the stables will be okay without me. You just make sure you take good care of your squirrel, hmm? He's special."

She gives me a wink, then eases the ring into my hand. With that, she clutches the fox to her chest, gives the room one last look, and disappears through the doorway, gripping Samuel's arm for stability as they hobble into the hall. The door clicks shut behind them, and then there were four.

"So?" Dalton says.

I open my palm and look down at the ring. "I mean . . . she really seemed like she wanted me to have it, so it's okay, right?"

"No, not the ring, bones. Will you marry me? I'm dying, here." He looks up at me, with all the hope in the world shining in his eyes.

Does he not know? Is he so unaware that there is only one answer to that question?

"Yes," I say with a roll of my eyes. "Of course I'll marry you. Now slide this ring onto my finger so we can celebrate!"

The ring eases over my finger, and it's a near perfect fit. It's a touch loose, but I'm dehydrated and starving to death after saving my boyfriend's life. Well, fiancé now. Once we're back on the road, eating and drinking as usual, I'll fluff up a little and it will fit just fine.

I look at the ring and smile.

A loud knock comes from the foot of the bed, and I finally remember our single remaining audience member. I rise from Dalton's lap and step around the bed. The mother lies on her side, still attached to the chair by her ankles. Her wrists are nearly free, and the remaining eyelid speculum fell off when she crashed to the floor. She still can't close that left eye, though. The tattered skin already looks dead and useless.

Dalton steps around me and rights the chair, then ties her wrists a little tighter. She screams something around a gap in the pillowcase, but we still can't understand her.

"Have you heard of the Halloween Harvesters, lady? Do you know who we are and what we do?" Dalton motions for me to join him in front of the woman. His arm glides around my bare waist, and he dips his face toward my breast, taking my left nipple into his mouth with a groan. When he breaks suction, he gives the tightened peak a little nip, and I moan. "We get off on this shit. The torture. The blood. But we especially enjoy it when our victims deserve it. You destroyed your family because of your obsession with grief, and now we're here to destroy you."

The woman begins nodding and crying, and my stomach sinks. She almost looks relieved. Dalton steps forward and yanks the pillowcase from her mouth.

"Yes," she says, but it's more croaked than spoken. "Send me to be with my son. If he's truly gone, I want to be where he is."

My shoulders droop. "Well, fuck. That takes all the fun out of it."

"No it doesn't." Dalton shakes his head and smirks down at the woman before stuffing the pillowcase into her mouth again. He places his hands on her shoulders and looks right into the eye she can't close. "Think about it, bones. If there is a god, would he allow this creature to recline in paradise after what she's done? No, I don't think he would. I think he'd probably stick her in a place where she would forever be separated from the child she refuses to let go of. She'll be locked in a pit where she can't even rely on delusions to comfort her."

The woman's eyes widen as that possibility confronts her. The panic is sweet, beautiful, and immediate. Gone is her reconciliation with death. Now she thrashes against the restraints and strains until the veins bulge from her neck.

Much better.

"I think we're ready to begin now," I say to Dalton.

He melts my insides with a devilish grin as he unfastens his belt. "Way ahead of you."

We both finish stripping down to our skin. What we're about to do is going to get messy, and our wardrobes are already so limited. We set our things off to the side so that they won't get bloody, and then we return to the bed.

Dalton holds the knife toward me. "He should be first so that she's forced to watch. A kindness for him, but hell for her. If she even has a feeling bone in her body."

He wants me to take the quick kill so that he can have the torture, which is fine by me. I don't take issue with the murder part, but I'm more interested in the body parts afterward. Our symbiotic relationship is pretty great.

Well, for us. Not so much for our victims.

But as I slide onto the bed, it seems I won't have to kill at all. The husband has already expired. I'm only mildly disappointed, though, because I get a better idea.

Over the man's body, I pull Dalton in for a kiss. His mouth moves to my neck, and as he bathes my skin in sensual, hungry kisses, I whisper in his ear so that only he can hear.

"He's already dead, but she doesn't know that. Play along."

He growls against my skin. "Your wish is my command," he whispers back.

I move to the head of the bed and straddle the man's face. Dalton opens his mouth to argue, but then he remembers that this mouth isn't experiencing me at all and will never experience anything again. It's all an act to psychologically torture his bitch of a wife.

"Fuck, for a dying man, he sure is hungry for good pussy," I say as I tweak my nipples and look right into the woman's face. "Is that why you were so afraid for him to see my body? Were you scared he might realize what a hag his wife is?"

She screams and throws her body forward, but Dalton stuffed the gag back into her mouth, so at least it's muffled. He also moved the chair against the foot of the bed so that she couldn't topple to the floor again. This is one performance we won't allow her to miss. And we value audience participation.

Dalton moves closer to me, sitting up on his knees beside me as his hand caresses my ass and guides the gentle rock of my hips. Grinding on a dead man's face creates an interesting sensation. His skin no longer produces warmth, creating a steadily cooling sensation against my pussy. I imagine what it will feel like when Dalton replaces that death chill with his living heat, and it's enough to make me clench.

"When the woman isn't a raging cunt, no amount of skin can tear a loyal man's eyes away from her. You never have to fear that from me. I worship you, bones, and no one will ever tempt me to stray."

"You don't have to fear it either, Dalton. I said yes to you because I say no to everyone else. Always." I rock my hips faster. "Only you."

He sits up straighter and fists his cock, stroking to the same rhythm. "How does he feel beneath you?"

The woman screams behind the gag.

"I'm close already, but I want you to make me come." I trace along the man's midsection with the blade. "Let's see what's inside first, though."

Without any more fanfare, I sink the knife into his abdomen. The metal slides through skin, and without any tensing muscles to provide added resistance, it's like pushing through a chuck roast. I grip the handle and brace myself, yanking back with each forward drive of my hips. My tempo slows, dragging out the promise of sweet release. Blood cascades over the side of the separated skin and sloshes against Dalton's thigh. He drags his hand through the crimson puddle and keeps stroking his cock.

The woman finally works the gag free. "Please just let me go. I'll be a better person. I will let go of my son, I promise! He's dead, and I know that now. You helped me understand."

"Bitch, you can plead all you want, but nothing is stopping this," Dalton says.

With blood coating his cock and the promise of more on the way, he loses control. His hand travels across my scalp. He grips my hair at the back of my head and squeezes until each root screams in ecstasy. My eyes practically roll in my head. I drive my hands into the man's abdomen and revel in the slippery texture of organs and tissue as an orgasm builds low in my belly.

Dalton yanks my head toward his stiff cock and forces my lips over the bloody coating. I barely have time to protect my teeth as he rams himself to the back of my throat.

A low growl rumbles within his chest. "You like it when I choke you with my dick, don't you?"

It's impossible to reply with his dick blocking my windpipe, but he never expected a response. That much is clear as his head tips back and he fucks my face a little harder.

The woman has had all she can stand. The legs of the chair grate against the floor as she scoot-hops toward the door. I don't know what she expects to do when she gets there, but she's giving it her very best.

Dalton pulls himself from my mouth and hurries to stop her. Gripping the chair back, he tips her backward and wobbles her to her starting position. Personally, I'm getting bored with the audience.

"Let's finish her off so we can finish each other. Please?" I say with a perfect pout.

That sends her into a tirade of screams and wails.

"How'd you want to do it?" he asks.

I reach back into the man's insides, claw past a wall of muscle, and grip a rope of intestines. "I think I have an idea."

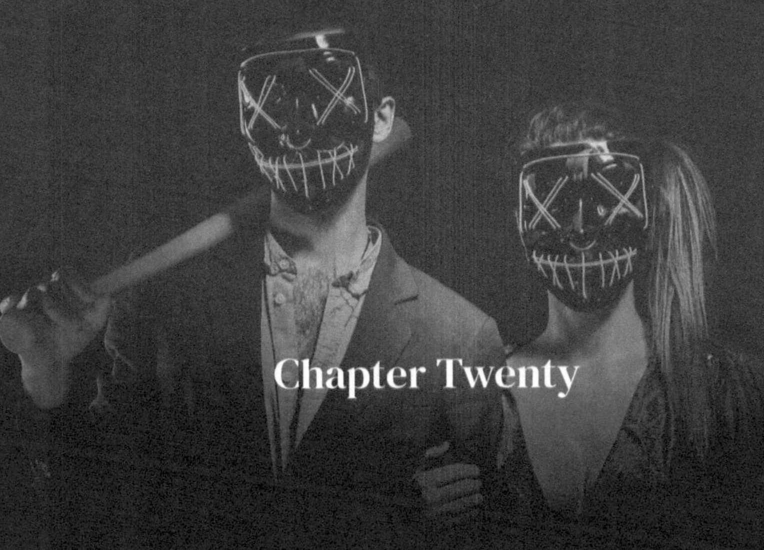

# Chapter Twenty

### Dalton

The intestines prove too slippery and fragile. They tear and slide out of our fingertips each time we wind them around her neck or an appendage. I'm currently sitting on the woman's back as she flails and cries beneath me. By the time we abandon the intestines, my dick is flaccid and flopping between my legs, and she's covered in shreds of blood and human tissue. It doesn't change the fact that she has to die, though, and I really like Rayna's plan, so I look around for an alternative.

My gaze settles on a landline phone on the bedside table. It's not a cordless model, so there are two cords to choose from. "Bones, over there," I say with a nod toward the cords.

She sees what I mean and hurries to retrieve what we require. When she reaches my side again, she secures the woman's appendages as I hold them in place. Now for the kicker.

"Just like we practiced," I say as she loops the second

cord around the woman's throat and attaches it to the hog tie. When she sits back with a grin, so proud of her work, I'm practically beaming with pride myself. "Beautiful. Now every time she relaxes, she'll start choking herself a little more."

She pats the woman's head, then stands up. "She won't be able to watch us if she's on the floor, though."

"Then I guess we fuck on the floor." I shrug. "Wouldn't be the first time."

"Yeah, the bed is kind of messy, what with his guts everywhere. Not that fucking in a pile of guts would be a turnoff."

"Speak for yourself," I mutter as I rise to my full height and pull her into my arms.

The blood has begun to dry, so we stick together wherever we touch. My hands stutter as they slide down her sides and land on her hips. She's so beautiful. And she's all mine.

"I love you, bones."

The woman whimpers at our feet as her body begins to grow tired in that position.

Rayna drops to her knees in front of me, aiming her ass toward me as she faces the woman. Their noses are inches apart as she turns and looks at me over her shoulder. "And I love you. Now get down here and make me come before she dies."

"Wouldn't want her to miss that. It's the most spectacular thing I've ever experienced."

I drop to my knees behind her and stroke myself as I stare at the enticing sight before me. Her full ass begs to be spanked and squeezed. Just beyond her, the woman is losing her fight. Panic lights her eyes as she spares a millimeter of space to relax. That brief respite cost her some rope, and the thin cord digs into her neck a little more. Not enough to kill her yet, but enough to let her know it's coming.

The visual stimulus is enough to get me going, and I push inside Rayna's warmth. A long, low moan rolls out of her mouth and slaps the woman in the face. The woman grunts and tries to turn her head, but that movement only tightens death's grip.

Rayna must be enjoying it as well. With every whimper from the woman, her pussy clenches around my throbbing cock. Fuck, she's so wet.

Despite having emptied my balls a ridiculous amount of times, I'm too close already. We still have a ways to go, and I don't want to finish before the main event. She's just too perfect in this position. Every forward thrust pulls more pleasure out of me, and it's all connected to her. After only a few minutes, I need to switch positions.

I ease out of Rayna and roll her onto her back, angling her so that she can still watch the suffering. Once I get her on her back, I grip her thick thighs and pull her closer. She's like a perfect little fuck doll, so compliant and willing. She can be bossy in her own right, but she knows when to hand the control to me, like right now.

Hushed groans and grunts escape from the woman as she loses more line. She's trying so hard to hold it together and remain calm.

I'm not. I'm done holding back.

"Use me, Dalton," Rayna whispers. "Fuck me like I don't matter."

With fucking pleasure.

I force myself inside her, earning a pained yelp, but I hear the pleasure in that sound. She turns her head to the side to continue witnessing the woman's demise as I raise her hips and slide my hands under her lower back to give me the leverage I need. In my grasp, she's so small and fuckable.

I pump her on my cock, harder and faster. She rises onto her toes to give me a better angle, and I rail her as we watch death creep closer beside us. Rayna drives her hand between her legs. Her fingers move in a blur as she massages her swollen clit. As her thighs begin to shake, I'm unsure if it's from an impending orgasm or impending paralysis as I pound her spine out of alignment.

"I'm so fucking close," Rayna grits out between her clenched teeth.

Question answered.

My balls draw up at the promise of her pleasure, but I'm still not ready. Not yet.

I focus on the ceiling, keeping my tempo steady for her sake. I keep fucking her brutally for mine. The ceiling is the safest place to look, though. If I see the way her breasts sway with each forceful thrust, I'll lose all control. She's so beautiful that it hurts sometimes.

Rayna's pussy starts clenching in a rhythm, and we're out of time. As she begins to shake, so does the woman beside her, though for a very different reason. Rayna is busy living while that bitch is busy dying.

Witnessing death as Rayna begins to orgasm—this is my magnum opus.

This is what we've been moving toward, and it's beautiful.

Veins bulge in the woman's neck as her head is held at that awful, awkward angle. They thump in a desperate ragtime beat as the circuits disconnect in her brain. The rapid tempo is so similar to the clench-clench-clench of Rayna's pussy that I'm almost certain we're all connected in this moment.

"I'm going to fill you, bones. I can't hold back."

Rayna cries out and lets go fully. Come jets from me, unloading all of my pleasure deep inside her perfect pussy as her orgasm overcomes her. The scrabbles of a thrashing body in its death throes provide the perfect accompaniment as we ride out our pleasure together.

When I've finished, I brace myself above Rayna and look into her eyes. I have never loved anything the way I love this woman. She makes my happiness possible.

I lean down and place a gentle kiss on her lips. She sighs against my mouth, and we breathe each other in as our victim ceases to breathe at all.

"It's done," I say. "We did it. We beat them."

She smiles up at me and takes a deep breath. "The Halloween Harvesters strike again."

# Epilogue
## Three Months Later

### Dalton

I stand at the hotel window and look into the snow-covered courtyard. Rayna wanted to go north for winter, so we hoofed it back up to New York to stay for a bit. We still move around a lot, just to avoid drawing too much attention, but we tend to stick around one spot for a week at a time. It makes Rayna's oddities business a little easier to operate.

She got the idea when we were driving out of Oak Hollow. When we got back to our car, Samuel had fixed it up and loaded it down with gifts. The entire backseat had been filled with all sorts of unique taxidermy pieces. It was more than we could tote around, so Rayna decided to sell some of it.

Well-done taxidermy goes for a fucking premium. Who knew?

Now she's turned it into a money-making machine. With the profits from one piece, we typically have enough to pay for our living expenses for a few weeks. We've even managed to stash away a small nest egg. We're saving for an RV.

"What do you think about this one?" Rayna shoves her phone into my face.

I pull the device back so that I can see whatever it is she's trying to show me. It appears to be a wedding dress made of latex, but it's been designed to look like sewn-together chunks of human skin.

I clear my throat. "I think it's unique, but you'd never be happy with the facsimile. You'd want the real thing."

"You're right." She lowers the phone and sighs. "I feel like I'll never find the perfect dress."

"The dress doesn't have to be perfect. It's just going to end up on the floor."

She swats my chest and laughs. "I still want to feel pretty on my wedding day."

"We'll be the only ones in attendance."

"Exactly. I want to look good for my man." She stands on tiptoes and plants a kiss on my cheek.

I pull her against my side and smile as I stare out the window again. Never in a million years did I ever think I'd propose. Now it seems like the best decision I could have made.

The clouds break enough to let a bit of sunlight catch in the diamonds perched on Rayna's hand. Her vintage ring gets compliments galore. I felt weird about it at first, but seeing how much she loves it lets me know it was meant to be. Nothing I came up with would have had quite the punch. Or the memories behind it.

We've watched the Florida papers for any mention of what occurred in Oak Hollow, but we've seen nothing. The town's website was quietly shuttered one night, and we haven't heard anything since. Wherever Samuel and his grandmother are, they made good on their promises. They didn't return to Oak Hollow, and wherever they are, they're keeping their heads down and their mouths shut.

"We should start planning for next Halloween," Rayna says as she takes a seat in the chair by the window. Van Gogh stands on the small table beside her. "The killing was pretty great, but there wasn't enough of it. Now that we have a van, we gotta up our game."

That's another change. We've swapped the car for a van. It was white with no windows, which draws entirely too much attention, so we painted it a pretty shade of purple and emblazoned it with Rayna's business name: Beautiful Bones. Oddly, we get fewer looks than we did when it was white.

"Speaking of the van," I say, "I should probably bring in that lemur you were working on. Didn't you want to practice some more today?"

She nods. "Yeah. I'll never get good if I don't practice. Once I can touch up pieces, the next step is learning how to do it from start to finish. Let me throw on some shoes, and I'll come with."

We dress in coats and trudge into the winter wonderland. By the time we reach the parking lot, she's stopped no less than three times to make a snowball and throw it at me. I let her because it makes her laugh. I love that sound.

As we draw closer to the van, I spot a set of footprints around it. Despite the heavy snowfall a couple of hours ago, the tracks are crisp and clear. Someone's been snooping around.

"Bones, do you have your blade on you?"

She nods and pats her hip, taking note of the footprints.

I ready myself beside the van door as she holds the blade in her hand and prepares to attack. Gritting my teeth,

I grip the handle and pull. Rayna's hand lowers from its stabbing position, and her eyebrows pull together.

I step forward and look into the van. Nothing looks amiss; Rayna's lemur project still sits in a box on top of fifty other boxes, and nothing has been disturbed. But then, I see it.

"Mr. Fox?" Rayna whispers as she steps forward and plucks the familiar taxidermy creature from the floorboard.

A slip of paper flutters to the snow. I bend and pick it up.

It seems you two are doing well, and I'm happy for it. Grandmother wanted Rayna to have this. I promised I'd deliver it myself, so I'm making good on that promise. I had to go back to Oak Hollow to bury her, which means I broke the promise I made to you. I hope the gift on Mr. Fox's neck will make up for it. Rayna's is from my mother. Yours is from my father. I hope the wedding is beautiful. Thanks again.

I reach over and take the fox from Rayna. Attached to his neck is a small satchel, and something inside clinks around as I open it. I pour the contents into my hand, and Rayna gasps.

"Are those wedding bands?" she says. "What are they made from? Wood? Did Samuel carve these himself?"

I pass the note to her, and she takes a moment to read it.

As realization dawns, her mouth transforms into a wide grin.

"Oh, fucking *sick*, dude! He made wedding bands from their bones! Please tell me we can wear them when we get married. I know you didn't like Samuel, but—"

Shutting her up with a kiss is one of my favorite things to do. I pull back and grip her face in my hands. "I didn't like the thought of losing you. Now I know nothing can tear you away from me. You're mine, and that will never change. If you want these to be our wedding bands, then I want that too. If you want Samuel to be my best man, we'll start hunting him down. Whatever you want, bones, it's yours."

"With a little convincing, sometimes." She smirks and grips my dick through my pants. Then her smile falls. "I'm sad to hear about his grandmother, though. Now he's all alone. I hope he finds his someone special someday."

Yeah, it can be a lonely life to be so deranged and have no one to share it with. I hope he finds someone too. He deserves to know the happiness I've found.

I take Rayna's hand in mine as we start back for the hotel's warmth. "Now, let's get you inside. We've got a Halloween wedding to plan."

Make sure you check out all of Lauren's dark-romance hitchhiker standalones in the Ride or Die series! These books can be read in any order.

*Hitched*: Books2read.com/Hitched
*Along for the Ride*: Books2read.com/MFMHitchhiker

*Driving my Obsession*: Books2read.com/
DrivingmyObsession
*Across State Lines*: Books2read.com/AcrossStateLines

If you need a palate cleanser, consider Lauren's dark rom-com series.

*Sinners Retreat*: Books2read.com/SinnersRetreat
*Slay Ride*: Books2read.com/SlayRide
*Ship Happens*: Books2read.com/ShipHappens
*Slaughter Park*: Books2read.com/SlaughterPark

Or something from Lauren's dark-lite selection.

*Stranger Session*: Books2read.com/StrangerSession
*Her Fantasy*: Books2read.com/HerFantasy
*Last Mistake*: Books2read.com/LastMistake
*Protect Me*: Books2read.com/ProtectMeNovella
*Dark Decisions*: Books2read.com/DarkDecisions

# Connect with Lauren

Don't miss a thing from Lauren Biel! Check out all of her books, social media connections, and other important information at Campsite.bio/LaurenBielAuthor and Lauren Biel.com

# Acknowledgments

To my VIP gals (Jessie, Nikita, Lexi, Grace, and Kim), LOVE YOU!

Thank you to my husband, who loves me even when I let my intrusive thoughts win . . . again. I love you and Whitney (owner of Bayside Books LLC in Panama City) like Rayna loves Van Gogh.

Brooke, my editor, my taxidermy queen, I literally couldn't have done any of these books without you!

High honorable mention to the incredible Nowhere Eternity and Katrina Medina because if they didn't agree to voice this, I wasn't even going to write it!

Finally, my mother, because she recently said I don't put her in any of the acknowledgements. Enjoy this weird taxidermy smut, Mom! But . . . don't actually read this.

Thank you to my valued Patrons. Your contribution helped make this book happen!

Raquel O, Samantha H, Clare, SimplyDevine, Hollie C, Samantha, Tanja, Jessica D, Stephanie R, Kelle T, Ashley M, Laura F, Kim R, Curvy Pear, Ashley S, Rebecca C, Kaat, Lauren K, Kimberly G, A.Reads, Samantha O, Cplay,

Danielle N, Sunshine_the_Bookie, Sara M, Harley B, Heather M, Bonnie F, Marguerite, Courtney R, Vikki S, Amanda T, Lisa W, Court's Bookshelf, Nicholetta88, Emily S, Sheena E, Queen Ilmaree, SerenaLorraine, Heather S, Jennifer S, Just Jen Here, Mikasa_Kuchiki, Jada W, Briyanna M, Jesi D, Charmaine B, Michelle, Christy P, Callie K, Arnica S, Maxine T, Alexandria R, Leslie W, Marisa K, Smitty, Brooke, Mandy G, Bailey A, Anna S, Shelby F, Tiannah J, Sharee S, Courtney P, Kristiana B, Vero A, Chelle, Sara S, Samantha R, Jessica G, Kimberly S, Tabitha F, JesStenger, Joanna, Nicole M, Eugenia M, Nineette W, BoneDaddyAshe

# Also by Lauren Biel

To view Lauren Biel's complete list of books, visit: https://laurenbiel.com/laurenbielbooks/

# About the Author

Lauren Biel is the author of many dark romance books, with several more titles in the works. When she's not working, she's writing. When she's not writing, she's spending time with her husband, her friends, or her pets. You might also find her on a horseback trail ride or sitting beside a waterfall in Upstate New York. When reading her work, expect the unexpected. To be the first to know about her upcoming titles, please visit www.LaurenBiel.com.